WHERE THE STARS HIDE

PATRICIA GULZAR

Book Cover by Madli Silm

Interior Illustrations by Gabrielle Solange

Song Lyrics by Gabrielle Solange

1st edition 2023
ISBN 979-8-9887150-0-9
Patriciagulzar@gmil.com
Write The Truth Prodcution

To my best friend, Gabrielle Solange,
who made it her dream to see my story
finally come to light.

One

I'd only seen an uncaged bird twice in my life. Running into the woods behind our house, I slipped on something, falling, and there it was: small and brown, lying in the dirt. I reached out to touch what I thought was a toy, but the slight movement of its chest made me jerk back. It was unheard of to see a bird outside, free. No crowd of children to push through like for the hawk exhibit, no velvet rope between it and myself like with the stuffed owls behind glass. It wasn't one of many trained cranes performing for food. This was just a single, lonely bird that twitched every few moments. I thought it was sleeping, ignoring the flies and the smell. I found a small box and made a bed of grass for it, excited to show my mother.

But when I did, she jumped back, smacking it out of my hand. I cried like most five-year-olds would when something spectacular is taken away, even if that thing is dead.

The second one still feels like something out of a dream. My house was the last stop on the bus ride home from school, and one day, through the window, I saw the bird perched on our mailbox. I thought maybe Grandpa had put something out for decoration until it stretched its wings.

"No way," I said, jumping out of my seat. There was a tingle in my chest, the same one I would get when catching some blue in the sky between the clouds. I was ready to believe it was a ghost as I made my way to the front of the bus. The doors couldn't open soon enough. I quickly stepped off, hoping I wasn't the only one seeing it. I was afraid to blink, fearing it would disappear. It was a crimson-feathered, black-faced, yellow-beaked creature, small enough to hold in my palms. Where did it come from? I stopped myself when I realized I was getting too close.

"Rita, Rita!" I whispered, trying to signal to my friend as she stepped off the bus behind me. I stayed fixated on the animal, letting its beauty quench my desperate need for something more. I reached for Rita as she started toward my house. I breathed in slowly, trying to quiet my heartbeat from scaring the bird away.

"Oh, Mae! Why couldn't your grandfather build your house closer to the road?" she complained as the bus drove off, kicking dust into the air.

"Rita, are you seeing this?" I called again, trying to keep sight of the creature. But once the dust cleared, my bird was gone.

"Seeing what?" Rita looked over at me.

"There!" I pointed, finding the red against the gray clouds. Rita joined me to see for herself, but the bird was gone for good.

"A cardinal, a red cardinal, was sitting right there on my mailbox." I'd recognized the bird from a book I'd found. I took a few steps as I scanned the sky, seeing if it was still nearby. "There was a cardinal. It was here seconds ago!"

"Really? I didn't see anything."

"I promise I saw it."

"Okay," Rita said with a tight smile as she turned to walk towards my house.

"It was there, I promise!" Then I stopped, quieting my voice. "That was incredible,"

I kept my eyes on the horizon, squinting and searching, but there was nothing. That wasn't the first time I had claimed to see something that hardly existed. From time to time, I would see a strange animal around my house. I learned to stop telling people because they always thought I was lying. I'd seen a rabbit once, and a chipmunk twice— though it could have been the same chipmunk. My parents were rarely around, so they never saw anything other than the dead bird I had brought them. They just ignored me if I mentioned seeing animals. And my friends—well, the people at school, anyway—just made fun of me. The only person who would take me seriously was Grandpa. He was outside as much as I was and saw animals sometimes, too; but he wasn't known for his sanity.

"Mae!" Rita called, pulling my attention away from the sky. "Come on, let's get this hike to your house over with." Rita threw her schoolbag over her shoulders. I looked defeatedly at the mailbox, placing my hand where the bird had stood, and then I followed Rita home.

We made it to the rocky white driveway that led into the woods. My house was far from the main road, hiding behind trees, causing visitors to miss us easily. I wouldn't blame anyone who believed we were keeping secrets, living so far from the city.

"I thought your grandfather would pick us up from school today.

If my mother finds out I took the city bus, I'll never hear the last of it," Rita said, gripping the straps of her bag under her arms. I was supposed to say something like "Your mom will get over it." But I was staring at my palms, rubbing my fingers against them, remembering the first time I'd touched the feathers of that dying bird.

"Mae?" Rita called. "Lost in the clouds again?" I looked up, realizing she wasn't in front of me anymore.

"Huh?" I said, looking back to find her. Rita had stopped walking, waiting for me to respond.

"Yeah, your mom will get over it, I'm sure," I replied.

"Okay, what's wrong? Are you thinking about that bird?"

"Nothing, I was just…thinking. Anyways, let's get this hike over with." I smiled and walked ahead. Above the path that led home were arched, tangled, bare branches of trees shielding us from the sun. They were nice to have when Eradeem's weather became sweltering, which was most days. Pebbles crunched under our feet as we continued up the hill to my house, making the trek more brutal than it needed to be. Rita dragged her feet, breathing heavily and sweating. I set my book bag in front of her. "Here," I said, kneeling. "Put some of your books in my bag so you don't pass out."

"Please!" Rita dropped her bag like it was a boulder. I took a couple of her books and a camera.

"What's this for?" I asked, rotating the camera before adding it to my bag.

"It's for a side project. I want to get some photos of myself as I start my change. I thought of it when my Abnormal started."

"Ooh, let me see. Did it change much?"

"No, it won't change that fast. I just got it this morning." Rita tucked her straight black hair behind her ear and pulled down her collar, exposing a dark gray, veiny mark the size of an apple. It was more noticeable against Rita's olive skin than the Abnormal I had seen on my dad or the one that would appear on me. Our dark skin obscured the Abnormal from afar, which was a positive, I guessed.

"I'm not looking forward to it," I said, grabbing my bag and continuing the walk.

"Really? You used to be so obsessed with Abnormal," Rita replied, fixing her collar. "It was like you couldn't wait until it happened to you or something."

"I wasn't obsessed. I was just curious. I don't know why people think curiosity is weird."

"They thought it was weird because you were against wearing anything to cover it up. You were like an advocate against wearing a flesh mask." Rita chuckled.

I tightened my lips. "That was last year, and it's over now," I said. "You don't have to keep talking about it. I thought you were coming over to work on your Lukenic project, not to take pictures of your neck."

"Well, yeah, the photos are a side project."

"For what exactly?"

"Just for me. I decided that I shouldn't wait to become a researcher when I can just do it now."

"You're taking a time-lapse of your Abnormal, but *I* am the weird one?"

"As I said, it's for myself. Anyways, do you think your grandfather would look at my project to see if it's good enough to get into Lukenic Academy?"

"I thought that's why you were staying over this weekend."

Rita turned her face, hiding the redness.

"You don't have to be embarrassed. I know how bad you want to get into Lukenic."

"No! I mean, yes. I want to get into Lukenic. But I came over because your house is more peaceful than mine. Plus, being in a house of Lukenic alumni could give me good luck."

Every year, academic leaders of Eradeem would come from Lukenic to accept two students in the eighth grade from every school. It was the only way to get into Lukenic with good grades alone. Rita was hoping to be one of those students that year from our school. As we continued walking, up ahead, pebbles crunched against the driveway as a black car approached us from my house. We both let it pass. Its shiny rims and body seemed untouched by the dust. I tried to get a look at who was in the car, but the windows were tinted black.

"Who's that?" Rita asked. "One of your grandpa's scientist friends? That's a nice car."

"No one I know," I said, looking back as the car turned onto the main road. "It's nice you think of Grandpa as good luck, though."

"He's the only Lukenic alumnus I know other than your parents, and he's always around. So, it's better than nothing," Rita responded.

The dark color of my roof peeped through the naked tree branches as we approached. Once we reached the edge of my driveway, Rita gasped for air, letting her bag hit the ground.

"How...are you... not... tired!" Rita panted.

"Less studying, more outdoor-ing. Therefore, you get to go to Lukenic, and I get to go to normal school."

"I haven't...been accepted...yet."

"Who's that?" I said, walking closer to the house.

Both of my parents were in front of the house talking with a couple of men.

"I thought your parents were gone until next month," Rita stated, trying to stand up straight.

"Yeah, so did I."

I took a couple of steps, focusing on the men my parents were with, both in all-black uniforms with the lower parts of their faces and heads covered. Rita's jaw was slightly dropped.

"Why are Vigilant officers here?" she asked.

We looked at each other as if we both knew what had happened. The Vigilant would only show up to take someone away. We continued walking toward the house until my dad noticed us. As one of the men left, I picked up speed to, avoiding eye contact with the Vigilant as Dad took me in his arms.

"Mae Flower!" he said, kissing my forehead.

I pulled back to see his face since it had been a while since I'd last seen him, but his eyes were swollen from tears. "Let's go inside," Dad said, signaling Rita to follow. Mom stood on the porch watching us. Her arms were folded tightly under her chest as the Vigilant continued talking. The door closed behind us, and I immediately scanned the room for Grandpa.

"What's going on?" I asked, letting my book bag slide down my back to the floor. Grandpa's glasses were sitting on the coffee table in the living room. They were usually there when he was taking a nap on the sofa.

"So," Dad began, sitting at the kitchen table. He leaned forward, running his hands against his face and hair, then resting his chin on his knuckles.

"Is this about Grandpa?" I asked. Dad stared off. He was almost frozen for a moment.

"Mae, I know this is most difficult for you. You were the closest to him, and—"

"Does…" I interrupted but then paused. I didn't want to ask, but I had to. I'd spent the entirety of last year fearing this moment—that I'd come home one day and learn Grandpa had been taken away.

"Does it have something to do with me?" I made myself finish, dreading the answer.

"Mae, no!" Dad said immediately. "It has nothing to do with you."

"That's not very convincing, after everything that happened last year!" I yelled, feeling my voice cracking. "You said they were going to remove him if I didn't stop talking about his stupid star research."

"Mae," my father stopped me. "I promise! It's not about you. I've been hearing great things from your teachers about your improvement."

"But I'm the one who got him in trouble!" I cried, looking over at Rita, who was staring at the both of us, squeezing her school bag to her chest. Dad signaled to me. He took my hands and looked into my eyes, which had filled with tears.

"It's not your fault. You were behind in your education because Grandpa filled your head with all that star stuff and Abnormal theories. He is the one who kept you out of school for years, making us think he had permission. He influenced you a lot, but this has nothing to do with you."

I lifted my gaze to my dad. I tightened my lips.

"Why did they take him, then?"

Dad opened his mouth to speak, but his eyes wandered behind me instead.

"You don't need to worry about that, Mae. Grandpa's going to be fine," my mother said. I turned around to see her standing by the door near Rita.

"You guys aren't going to tell me, then!"

"Mae, we aren't one hundred percent sure what's going on," Mom said.

"Well, what did the Vigilant say? Who told them to arrest him? And what are you guys even doing here? You must have known this would happen!"

"MAE!" Mom's voice overpowered mine. "Take Rita upstairs to your room; we will talk about this later." And like that, it was done. The conversation was over, and Mom left.

"Dad!" I called, looking over at him. He was always too gentle, but still, I hoped he might stand up to her.

"We can talk about this later, Mae," Dad said.

I ran upstairs to my room, throwing my bag onto the bed. Rita followed, and as soon as she entered the room, I slammed the door, making sure it shook the house.

Both of my parents were usually away from home working as biologists for a government-owned company called IRRAT. My grandfather used to be a scientist, too, until he was forced into early retirement because of his controversial studies. Everyone grew up believing that stars were just make-believe, existing only in old stories. The only consistent things in our sky were clouds.

We could feel the sun, and sometimes we could even see the moon. But never stars. So, since no one had ever seen a star, that was proof it wasn't real. Grandpa always taught me that stars were real; however, teaching children that they existed was treated as child abuse. Until the prior year, I didn't care what people said or thought of my grandfather. He'd dedicated his life to proving the existence of stars. He would say, just because we couldn't see them wasn't proof, that they didn't exist.

It seemed like the only person who supported my grandfather's research was me. My family threatened with removing Grandpa from our home if he didn't stop teaching me nonsense. The scientific community insisted Grandpa's studies were based on fantasy, not logic. So, the year I started eighth grade, I had no choice but to change my ways.

"They're barely here, and this happens!" I shouted.

"Mae, calm down; I'm sure he is going to be okay," Rita said.

I sat at my desk in the corner of the room between my bed and window. My back was to Rita as I stared outside. I couldn't help but blame myself. How could I not? I should have just done the work I was assigned at school the first time, listened to what I was told the first day, and taken an interest in things my classmates were into.

Kids laughing at me when I talked about my grandfather's star research had been hard to deal with, but being someone I was not was more difficult. Still, I tried as hard as I could. I had spent that whole year attempting to stay away from Grandpa. It was hard living with someone and trying to keep my distance from them. Especially because, other than Rita, Grandpa was my best friend.

"What else could it be, if he wasn't arrested because of me?" I whimpered.

Rita sat on my bed and took in a deep breath for me. "You're the person who has been around him the most, but I don't think you should blame yourself. It could be anything. Did you notice any strange behavior from him lately?"

I pulled my feet up onto the chair, resting my chin on my knees. The window beside my desk was large, stretching from floor to ceiling. Looking into the woods helped loosen the muscles in my shoulder. My mind was always clearer sitting there. There was a view of this path that led farther into the woods behind our house, where my grandfather's lab was. I'd see Grandpa when he left to go out to his base to be alone or work on a personal project. Since I had started school, he hardly went to his base. He focused his free time on me. But there had been something different about him for the last few months.

"Wasn't there an announcement at school about a curfew change?"

I asked Rita.

"Yeah, I think the youth curfew is eight p.m. now; why?"

"It's just..." I started, then stopped myself, knowing how I was going to sound.

"So..." I began, turning my chair to look at Rita. "Grandpa had been going out to his base more lately."

"You mean out in the woods."

"Yeah, but more than before." I paused, trying to collect my thoughts. "For a couple of months now. Every Friday night. Around midnight."

"Why would he do that?" Rita asked.

"I don't know. It's hard for me to sleep, so I always see him going out there."

"And what does that have to do with the new curfew?"

"The new curfew is only on Fridays, right?"

"So... you think the curfew has something to do with your grandpa?" Rita said as she raised her brow.

"Well, I don't know. I'm just trying to figure out why they took him. Maybe he was working on some secret project, or he found something. Something so dangerous that the curfew was moved."

"Could be," Rita said. "Maybe something he wasn't supposed to be doing. Like his research on *stars*; and if that's the case, maybe it's a good thing he was taken."

"What?" I shot back.

Rita's body stiffened. "Look, Mae," Rita stuttered, "I'm just saying that..." She paused, then took another deep breath.

"Your grandpa needs help."

I was stuck. I stared blankly, unable to believe she could say that to me.

"I thought you understood that," she continued. "Do you still believe in the stuff your grandfather talked about? You need to growup."

"I didn't say I did!" I snapped back. We were both silent.

This was a first, hearing Rita talk to me like this. She had always admired Grandpa, at least in front of me.

"Mae. I've always been on your side. I've taken up for you when people said horrible things about you and your family. So, don't treat me like this. At some point, you must realize that things are probably what they seem."

"Right," I said, turning back to the window, as my face dropped.

"Look, Mae, I'm not trying to hurt your feelings," Rita said, shuffling her bag of schoolwork onto the bed and taking another deep breath. "Okay, it's possible that the curfew change may have something to do with your grandpa getting arrested. I just don't want you to go back to how things used to be. You're finally doing better in school, you're making friends, and you're not struggling anymore. I just want you to be happy."

I pressed my lips together, slumping down in my seat. "I guess you're right." The three years of loneliness slammed against my memory like a bag of bricks. Since I was taught at home for the first five years of my education, I'd had no friends until I started school. I was weird, outspoken, and talked about stars a lot. I didn't know better.

I didn't know that I wasn't normal. I might as well have come from outside Eradeem. I had to let go of my grandpa's beliefs to become a better student, but it only left me feeling empty. Rita was right, except for the part about me being happy. Going to school was difficult, but at least I had Grandpa to come home to. Regardless of whether my grandpa was wrong about his research, I didn't want to regret not investigating why he was taken.

"Okay, just let me do this one thing, Rita. I'm more than likely going to Grandpa's base past curfew tonight. I won't be able to sleep if I don't. You don't have to come; you made it clear how you feel about Grandpa." Before she could respond, a knock came from the door and my dad's head peeked through the crack.

"Hey," he said with a low voice. "Just checking in with you guys."

"We're fine," I replied, jumping to my feet.

"Okay," he said, opening the door to step in. He pressed his lips together, glancing around the room. He hardly came into my room when he was home. Work took a toll on my parents. When they had a break to come home, they mostly slept.

"Oh," he said, looking over to the wall where my bed was. "Where's Grandpa's poster? You used to have it there." I looked over to what was now a poster of a boy group called Lost Generation.

"Someone from the school came by, so I took it down. I mean, I didn't put up Lost Generation because of that," I said, hesitating like an imposter. "Rita and I went to their concert a few months ago."

"Oh. Glad that you are enjoying your youth, honey." He nodded at the poster. "Your mom used to have this room set up just how yours is, except her walls were covered with boy bands and musicians." I looked at the one music poster and then the rest of my room. I had several sketches of animals I had posted, a string of lights that framed my bed and desk, some animal figures sitting on a bookshelf, and random plastic dots that glowed in the dark, covering the walls and ceiling.

"I guess I'm still a bit immature," I said, taking hold of my arm.

"No, I love it. It's just good to see you becoming a normal teenager." I didn't reply.

"Anyways," Dad started as he cleared his throat. "We are going to get Grandpa back. So don't you worry about him."

"Thanks," I said, still standing, shifting my eyes to Rita. I hoped he hadn't heard my plan to go to Grandpa's base tonight.

"Mr. Meadows," Rita said, "Dr. Cefend was planning to help me with a project to get into Lukenic. I wasn't sure if you might be available to look over it."

"Sure, I can do that, Rita. I know it can be stressful trying to get into that school," Dad said.

Rita's eyes widened as she scooted closer to the edge of the bed. "If you aren't too busy, that would be great."

"I'm pretty free for the rest of the day, so just come find me when you're ready."

"Okay, thank you, Mr. Meadows."

"All right," Dad said, glancing at me as he closed the door.

"Well, that worked out," I said.

Rita didn't respond. She grabbed her bag and walked over to the full-size mirror next to the door. She reached into her bag and pulled out a thin, clear baggie with a flat, translucent, palm-size square.

"Is that a mask piece?" I asked, walking over to get a better look.

"Yeah, my mother gave it to me this morning when I showed her my Abnormal. I thought I would try it out once I got to your house."

"Can I see it?" I asked. Rita handed it to me. I opened the bag, pulling out the artificial skin with the tips of my fingers, wobbling it in the air.

"Gross." I gagged.

"Stop it."

Rita sticked her palm out in front of me. I placed the mask skin in its bag and handed it back to her. "It's not gross; it's normal, Mae. You are going to have to use a mask sooner or later. In your case, probably later, since you have the mark of a toddler."

"I hope I never get the Abnormal," I replied. I pulled my collar away to look at the mark on my chest. It lay right above my heart. A dark gray spot that grew with age and usually stopped in puberty. It wasn't until I'd started school that I realized that mine was much smaller than my classmates'. Some of my classmates had marks the size of a handprint, while others reached down to their belly button. Mine was the size of a coin.

"It's not so bad having a small mark," I responded. "They said it would grow the more I was around other kids my age, but it hasn't changed much."

Rita took a hair tie from her bag, pulling her hair back in a ponytail. She placed the mask piece on her neck where her Abnormal was starting to grow. She patted it down with her fingers and then took a little makeup to help it blend in. Once she was done, she rubbed her fingers around it.

"Wow, it's gone," I said, touching her neck where the Abnormal was. "How does it feel?"

"A little weird, but I can get used to it."

"Yeah, but imagine when you need to use it all over your face."

Two

Rita joined my dad downstairs after applying her mask. The thought of going to Grandpa's base, especially alone in the dark, made my stomach uneasy. I wasn't sure what kind of answers it was going to provide. All I knew was that my parents were hiding something about why Grandpa was arrested and they weren't going to tell me. Dad was the easiest person to get information from, but since he was busy with Rita, I had to get Mom to throw me a bone. Mom was in her office like usual when she was home.

She was kneeling by the sofa that sat to the right of the room, looking through documents. Every surface was cluttered with files, notebooks with loose papers hanging out, and notes pinned to the wall. She hardly cleaned the office, and no one but Dad was allowed to touch anything. Even though the room was chaotic, she knew exactly where she'd left everything.

She normally went through all her papers trying to find some memos or notes she had taken, but this time something was different. She was shredding a lot of papers. She sorted through documents, keeping some and tossing others. I took a step into the room, trying not to startle her.

"Mom." It was a few moments before she noticed someone else was in the room.

"Yeah?" she mumbled as she continued working, not even giving me a glance. She fanned through the papers she was holding, dropped them, and continued with the next stack.

"So…" I paused, clearing my throat. "So, things seem kind of hectic," I said, walking into the room. I strolled around, looking at the walls where her notes were posted before finding a clear seat. "When did you and Dad get in town? You both look exhausted."

Mom's hair bun barely stayed together. It hung loosely behind her head and black strings of hair framed her face. Her lips moved without sound while she remained fixated on her documents. Her cheek revealed a torn mask slowly peeling, uncovering her real skin. My mother wasn't one to care about her appearance unless she was in public, so sometimes I got to see her Abnormal; but it seemed to be a bit different than before. It wasn't as brown. She finally looked over at me, realizing I was staring at the tear. She placed her palm on her cheek, rubbing it back into place.

"Yeah," she said, finally responding. "Just an hour before you got home. Neither Jace nor I got any sleep. Just trying to get home before the Vigilant."

She continued working, flipping through another bound document, pausing on a page. Her lips moved silently as her finger zipped across the paper. Her hand stopped at a point, and her eyes fluttered. Taking in a deep breath, she shook her head. "You idiot!" she scoffed, tossing the document into the trash. She stood, and she was trembling. "Leaving everything out in the open like this."

"Who?" I asked. But she didn't respond.

She was grinning, or maybe she was about to cry. "And let's not forget about Dad."

"Grandpa?" I continued, trying to ignore her frustration. "What about him?"

She moved around the room, grabbed more papers from the ground, and then paused, looking over at me as if just realizing I was there.

"Oh." She sighed, taking a seat at her desk for a break. Combing her fingers through her hair, she stared off, focusing on an empty place on the wall. "I'm working on getting him back home. So, don't worry about him. He'll be fine. He's getting the help he needs."

"Help? What do you mean, help?" I asked, narrowing my eyes.

"Mae, you know what I mean. Dad's been sick for years now. We should have gotten him help a long time ago." I really hoped she wasn't talking about a different kind of help. The kind provided for crazy people.

"Did something happen?"

"Mae, right now, I need to go through all these papers and clean up. We can talk about it another time." Which really meant she wasn't going to talk about it at all.

"Okay, fine," I said, standing up to leave, then pausing. "Do you need help cleaning up?"

"I don't care," Mom said.

The office was like another bedroom for her. A blanket and pillow sat next to me on the sofa, with clothes lying around the room. My mother often slept on the sofa when she was busy and would keep the door locked. I started taking the clothes to my parents bedroom. Grandpa didn't come in this room much, but whatever Mom was panicking about felt like it was connected to him somehow. Mom continued rummaging through papers, putting certain ones into a box and shredding the rest.

I walked over to the box, and something on top of the pile caught my eye. In the center of a paragraph, in bold letters, it read **Abnormal 3 Treatment.** I picked it up and skimmed through it, flipping the pages. I stopped at a picture of someone sitting on a bed nude, their back to the camera. Their skin was covered in discolorations that looked nothing like a usual Abnormal. The person in the picture was so skinny that it almost looked like they had an exoskeleton.

"Abnormal 3? What's Abnormal 3?" I said as Mom appeared in front of me, snatching the stack from my hands.

"What are you doing?" she said, taking me by my arm and leading me to the door. "You know what, Mae, I think I'm fine. Just go to your room, okay?"

"Wait, what's that all about?"

"It's nothing." She left me in the doorway.

"Mom, I can help!" I walked back into the room, looking for what I could do next.

"Mae, please!" Mom shouted, slamming her fist against the wall. "It would be best if you didn't help, do you understand?"

My mouth opened, but the words were delayed. Something in her eyes stopped me. Anger. Or was it fear?

"Okay," I replied.

I stood at the entrance, watching her for a moment, and then left. Dad was coming up the stairs as I walked into my room.

He probably heard Mom yelling. I closed my door but cracked it to peek out. He approached Mom's office and stood silently at the door. He leaned against the frame, shaking his head. "What was that all about?" he asked. I couldn't hear Mom's response.

"You are literally in here trying to cover your tracks as if that's going to change anything." His voice was intense yet quiet. I cracked the door further to hear better.

"If anything goes wrong, Jace," Mom hissed, "you better believe it won't be because of me."

"Really?" Dad said. "I'm the problem, huh? What about your dad and what you are doing to yourself, Elliaine?" He stepped into the office, away from my view.

Mom and Dad went back and forth arguing, but I couldn't make their words out. It wasn't long before Dad walked out, and Mom slammed the door behind him. I gently pressed my door shut. Something else was going on, and it had to be connected to why Grandpa was taken away.

I sat on my bed impatiently watching the clock; the second hand seemed to barely move. Rita was still with Dad working on her project. I pulled my books from my bag, hoping that doing homework would make nine p.m. come faster, but I couldn't focus. What was Abnormal 3 about? The picture of the diseased person kept popping into my mind.

I thought about what I might find at Grandpa's base. Before I'd started school, Grandpa was my teacher. I studied at home with him until I was ten. I didn't know it at the time, but home education was illegal. Grandpa thought it would be better if I got my education from him. Since my parents were rarely home, Grandpa was able to get away with it by making some excuse to tell them why I was not at school if they caught us. My parents never really questioned it, though, or asked me about what I was learning. They were so busy with their work they just thought Grandpa, being one of the top intellectuals in Eradeem, had it under control.

Every morning I would go out with Grandpa to his base in the woods. I would ask, sometimes, why I didn't go to a normal school. His response was always, "Because you're going to be different from the other kids." He used to tell me that my Abnormal would take longer to grow if I wasn't around other kids. I didn't think much of it at the time, but he was right. When I finally started real school, I was so excited; but it wasn't at all what I thought it would be. I got in trouble on my first day of fifth grade for leaving the classroom without permission, going to the bathroom without asking, and talking while the teacher spoke, even though I was only speaking about what they were teaching. I eventually learned the rules and followed them.

I'd met Rita, who helped me a lot, though I still got in trouble for just wanting to learn. Grandpa not allowing me to go to school my first five years felt like a big mistake. He wanted me to be different, but I was different in a bad way. I had the lowest grades for history and social science. Reading, and math were the only things I scored high in, yet no matter how hard I tried, I just didn't understand any of the other subjects.

I spent three years challenging my teachers because most of what they taught wasn't what I'd learned at home. It was in science that I got in the most trouble, especially if my teachers mentioned stars. I always seemed to ask too many questions or the wrong questions and barely passed the next grade each year, but I was sure it was because my teachers didn't want to deal with me again. It finally hit me last year that school wasn't a place to learn; it was a place to be taught what to think. I was warned that I would end up in a different institution if I kept disrupting the class. They knew it was because of Grandpa that I struggled, so they threatened to remove him from the house if I didn't comply.

I was pulled from my class an hour a day for tutoring and slowly began unlearning everything I had been taught at home. Grandpa used to say that challenging ideas was how society improved. That an unchallenged mind would forever be lost. He inspired me so much. He made learning feel exciting. I thought he was so amazing until I was forced to believe otherwise. I finally accepted what everyone said about him, that he was out of his mind. That he was a fading light, no longer in his glory days. Even the teachers attested to my Abnormal delay being due to my homeschooling. Your Abnormal development was a sign of a healthy child; at the same time, we were encouraged to cover it up in public.

I barely touched my homework assignment, thinking about what Mom was hiding. The evening could not come fast enough. I wanted to be sure that when I left, everyone would be asleep. The good thing about living out as far as we did was that most Vigilant didn't come around this area. There was only a slim chance I would be caught outside past curfew, especially in the woods; but I worried a bit that there might be patrol around because of Grandpa's arrest. I told myself that if I got caught, I would pretend I didn't know about the new curfew.

It was around eight p.m. when Rita finally came upstairs. I had given up on my homework and decided to search the house for some of Grandpa's notes. I was hoping to get a clue about what he was working on last. When Rita came through the door, I dropped Grandpa's work on the side of my bed.

"You were down there for a long time," I said.

"Yeah, I was done a while ago, but started talking to your dad about going to Lukenic."

"Oh, that's not surprising."

"You don't know how lucky you are to have alumni as parents. You don't have to work as hard to get in Lukenic as I do."

"Well, I'm apparently not good enough to go there at all, even with my parents' help."

Rita rolled her eyes as she took a seat on my bed. "Anyways, your dad was very helpful."

"I'm glad that you got what you needed," I said. "But even without his help, I know you could still get into Lukenic. You've been talking about it ever since I met you. No one wants it more than you; you deserve it." I squeezed my pillow against my chest, staring down to hide how I truly felt about her possibly leaving. Rita fell back onto my bed, looking up at me as she bit her bottom lip and sighed.

"I decided I will come with you tonight, since there's no stopping you."

"Really?" I said, straightening up from my seat. "So, what made you change your mind?"

"Because I wouldn't be a good friend if I let you go alone."

"Great!" I sighed, relieved that I wouldn't be by myself. "I'm glad you changed your mind. It means a lot to me, Rita."

Three

I heard something moving in the trees above us. Pointing my flashlight up, I searched the branches, but nothing was there. "Are you sure Vigilant don't come around this area?" whispered Rita from behind me.

"I never see them around here," I responded.

"Ouch." Rita grabbed hold of her bare arm after a scratch from a branch. "Someone really needs to clear this path better. I don't remember the trees being so thick like this."

"It's only because you can't see anything when it's dark." I pointed my flashlight back to the naked treetops, slowly moving it back and forth.

"What are you looking for?" Rita looked up to where the flashlight pointed as she pushed twigs and branches away from her face.

"I thought I heard something in the trees," I whispered.

"What on earth would be in a tree? A monkey?"

Lowering the light, I ignored Rita's comment. "Okay, we aren't very far. Just a little longer," I said, continuing on the path to Grandpa's base.

"Once we get there, we'll look around and then leave, right?"

"I want to look around first, but it might take a little while."

"What exactly are you expecting to find out here, Mae?"

What was I expecting? I didn't really know. All I knew was that Grandpa had spent his time here before he was arrested. I wondered if he had discovered something and was hiding it. I guessed it was also possible he really did just go mad.

My pace slowed at that thought. "I just want answers."

As we got closer, I could see my grandfather's base through the bushes. We walked from the woods to an open field, where Grandpa's small wooden cabin was. Three stone steps led up to a dark blue door. There were two windows on each side of the door, two in the back, and one window on each side of the house.

"He was definitely here today before they took him," I said, noticing that all the lights were on.

"You sure they don't know about this place?" Rita asked as we walked to the door.

"I don't think so. Unless my parents told them."

Inside, everything seemed normal; though, since starting school, I hadn't come out to Grandpa's base at all. It was more like a tiny home than a laboratory. I remembered doing eight cartwheels from one side of the house to the other when I was younger. Grandpa's desk sat a few yards away from the door against the wall. To the right of the door was a bed built into the wall, big enough for two to sleep; and on the other side was a square table against the window in the small kitchen.

Papers flooded every flat surface other than the floor; it wasn't as bad as my mother's office. It felt like Grandpa hadn't left and would be back any moment. I walked over to his desk, where a book had been layed open next to a notepad. It was a children's book he'd found a long time ago, written in a dead language Grandpa could read. I flipped to the cover, which was black with yellow circular drawings on it.

The title was in white words. I flipped through the pages, looking at the illustrations. Although I didn't understand the language, the pictures told a story. It was about a prince and a poor girl falling in love. There was a page that showed the girl near a cave where an ugly old man was. She had long, straight black hair that touched the ground, and her skin was dark. Some of Grandpa's gibberish notes were written in the book, but I couldn't make them out. I sat in his chair, looking over it, flipping through the pages.

I looked at Rita, who was lying down with both feet on the bed. She held up a large, white, cylinder-shaped paper bag.

"What's that?" I asked.

"I'm not sure, but there's another one in the kitchen," Rita said, pointing to the other side of the room. I walked over and picked it up. It was exactly like the one Rita had—a thin, white, lamp shade-looking thing. The bottom had a burned pad that was connected to the wires holding the paper lampshade as big as my head.

I rotated it and found a strange symbol on the other side. Two large bent triangles and two smaller triangles pointed at each other, with the shape of a crystal between it. Right below it was an upside-down trapezoid. Then I notice words written on the bottom from inside the cylinder in small script.

Ghost, bird, man, king
To Eradeem, the light they bring
They alone can bring back peace
Once beast beneath has been unleashed

"Does yours have words on it, too?" I asked Rita.

"Oh," Rita said, finding them. "I didn't notice."

"What's it say?"

King, man, bird, ghost
Hurt by who he loved the most
Cursed from birth our fate was sealed
To be healed by truth revealed

Rita read. "Did your grandpa make these?"

"I don't know," I said, taking a seat on the bed next to her. "I wonder what this symbol means."

A small bookshelf hung on the wall at the foot of the bed. There were plenty of nights I'd slept there, letting my toes hook to the bookshelf. A handsewn plush doll my grandmother made was sitting on the shelf between two books. Its long arms and legs hung out of a white lace dress with a soft pink tulle skirt. Ginger yarn hair framed a brown face with closed eyes.

"I thought I lost this thing," I said, pressing her against my face. "It was here the whole time." The coffee-dyed fabric scent opened old memories of Grandma. I used to watch her soak the cloth for the dolls she made in coffee to give them their brown skin. I fell on my side against the pillow, keeping my doll to my nose and my knees to my chest. Rita scooted to the other end of the bed, resting her head on the small bookshelf.

"Grandpa," I whispered to myself as I shut my eyes then fell asleep.

I dreamed Grandpa was in that room with us, trying to explain what had happened. When I opened my eyes, I couldn't remember what he'd said. Rita was gone. From the window, I could see the top of her head sitting outside by the door. I climbed out of bed to join her, keeping the doll with me. Rita was glaring at the sky.

"Do you see that over there?" Rita asked, pointing to where the sky was the darkest. I followed her hand to two faint, white dots against the darkest part of Eradeem's red gradient sky. "Yeah, I guess so," I said, squinting. "What is it?"

"I don't know, but doesn't it look like they're getting closer?"

I couldn't really tell. I was kind of surprised Rita wasn't mad that I'd kept her out so late. I wasn't even sure how long I had slept.

"I didn't mean to fall asleep on you like that," I said, joining Rita on the porch.

"It's fine; I didn't want to wake you up. Sorry about what I said earlier about your grandpa." She looked down at her hands.

"Oh," I said back. I guessed the guilt of my grandfather being gone had caught up to her.

Rita was a little hard at times, but she had never been too proud to apologize when she knew she'd hurt my feelings. She was the only one of my classmates who'd talked to me when I'd started school. In the back of my mind, I wondered why she wanted to be around me. Was it because of my family and their connection to Lukenic, or did she see me as a good person to be friends with?

"Rita?" I called.

"Yeah?"

"Why do you like me?" She looked over, wrinkling her brow.

"What do you mean?"

"Why, in the fifth grade, did you want to be friends with me?" I glanced over at Rita, trying to make eye contact, but she looked away. "Everyone thought I was weird, so why didn't you?"

"I mean, I *did* think you were weird," she replied. "But all that stuff you talked about was kind of interesting. I never heard anyone talk about it the way you did. I mean, I don't really believe in that star stuff, but it was something I hadn't thought about. And all the questions you used to bring up about wearing masks and the Abnormal. I guess I just enjoyed talking to you and listening to you. I mean, I thought you were smart, even though everyone else didn't."

She had never said anything like that before, so I was a little shocked.

"I thought maybe it was because of my family being Lukenic alumni?"

"What? I didn't even know that until last year, Mae."

"I liked how smart you were, too," I said. "Plus, you didn't treat me like everyone else."

"Well, I did feel bad for you, too. I figured if you had a friend, people wouldn't put you down so much."

"Yeah, that didn't work," I said. We both broke out laughing. It was good to know what she really felt.

"Rita, look!" I pointed at the light post behind her. A red cardinal seemed to appear out of nowhere, unless it had been sitting on the light post the whole time we were talking.

"What?" She turned to see. "No way. Is that a bird?"

"I told you I wasn't just seeing things," I said.

"How did it get here?" Rita said. "It's red, too."

"See, I told you," I said, standing.

I headed inside to get Rita's camera, but before I could, I paused at the open sky where the two dots had become three. The white lights were getting closer, as Rita had said, and two more appeared behind them. I ran inside, grabbed the camera, and quickly came back out. It wasn't long before we saw more lights. We watched them as a trail started to appear. I snapped a few photos of the sky and the cardinal, too, which didn't seem to be afraid of me.

Then it seemed as though one of the lights began to break from the path, coming toward us.

The closer it got, the more it began to take shape.

"Don't you think it's kind of weird how that one is heading our way?" Rita said.

"It is strange." We both looked at each other.

"Where are they coming from?" I said, watching them go from a round shape to oval.

"Wait," Rita said, glaring at the light. "It looks like those things we found inside. The paper-cylinder things." It started to float downward to us. I stood, grabbed my doll, and stuffed it into my large pant pocket. I put the camera in the other one. I crossed the open field to get a closer look until it was right above me. Rita followed but kept her distance.

The lantern seemed to stop suddenly, then floated straight down. I could see a fire inside slowly dimming. The closer it got, the more it looked just like the white lamps in my grandpa's base. I reached, and without much effort, it landed in my hands, and then the fire was gone.

I looked at Rita, whose mouth was slightly dropped as she walked over.

"This must be it," I said, turning the paper cylinder in my hands. "Grandpa must have been coming out at night because of this."

I looked for the message like the others had; and, on the bottom, it read,

Orient sky, ablaze with stellary fire
Sent to guide the flight
Journey through the night
Over mountains and mire

Rita read the message over my shoulder. "What does it mean?" she asked.

"I don't know."

"Do you think someone is trying to communicate with your grandpa?"

I looked back up as other floating lights crossed the sky. "I wonder why they are all lined up like that," I said as I laid the lampshade down and headed off to the woods, where the lights were coming from.

"What are you doing?" Rita shouted, taking me by the arm. "Are you crazy?"

"I'm not going that far. I just want to see where they're coming from."

"They're obviously coming from somewhere far away, Mae!"

I looked over to the wooded area before me, trying to imagine the distance of the lights.

"How far could it be if Eradeem's border is close by?" I turned to Rita, gasping. "Unless you think it's coming from beyond the wall, like from the desert or something."

"No way," Rita said, looking up and stepping back, trying to see the horizon. "I mean, it wouldn't be possible. Nothing's out there."

"Exactly, so it won't hurt to go see."

"That wasn't the plan, Mae. We were just going to check out your grandpa's base and go back to your house."

"Okay, I changed the plan. You stay here, and I will go far enough to see what I can see." I walked off to the woods.

"Mae, stop!" Rita shouted.

"You can come if you want, Rita," I shouted back, waving my hands. I didn't see what the big deal was. We were already out here; going a little farther out couldn't hurt. As I got closer to the other side of the field and headed into the woods, I looked back, hoping Rita was behind me, and she was.

"I'm only coming to keep you out of trouble, Mae," Rita yelled. I smiled and continued onward.

I had to admit I was relieved she was coming. Not only were we not allowed to be out this late, but we were never supposed to be this far away from the city. The trees were thicker here, causing the treetops to block out the night's red hue. It made it harder to see where I was going. I heard a flapping sound overhead. I stopped to see a dark silhouette moving on a branch above me. I took my flashlight, pointed it up, and found that same cardinal from before. I could feel it looking at me. Did cardinals attack, and was this one following me? I wondered.

"You could at least wait for me, Mae," Rita shouted. "I can't see you."

"Okay," I said, giving a heavy sigh. I could see through the top of the branches that new lights were still appearing.

"Hurry up, Rita!" I said as I started walking again. I picked up my pace as I saw another light appear from behind the others.

"Mae, stop. I told you to wait."

"I am," I shouted back, but I didn't stop. I didn't want to lose track of the lights in the sky, but then something caught my eye close to the ground nearby. A small green flash of light appeared in the woods.

"What the heck is that? More strange lights?" I took a couple of steps toward it, and I saw it again. It was a tiny, soft green flash in the air. I looked back with my flashlight to see if Rita was close. The sounds of her steps from behind encouraged me to keep going. I ran ahead into a cluster of lights. "Bugs?" I asked myself. They kept flashing on and off, appearing in different areas. It seemed like the closer I got, the easier it was to lose sight of the small green light. Then I saw another one flash, so I changed my direction slightly. I walked over, pointing my flashlight at it, but I saw nothing.

"Thanks for stopping!" Rita said from afar.

"Where is that coming from?" I asked myself, and there it was again, almost in front of me; but then, nothing. I walked over to that exact spot. "I swear I saw it." I moved my flashlight in the air but saw nothing. More appeared, coming from a tree, and then the ground, and then another out of thin air, shining in my face. One stayed in one spot on a tree, and kept going on and off. I got close enough, pointing, my flashlight at a little black bug. I watched it turn into that soft green glow again.

"That's incredible," I said, reaching to touch it. It seemed safe. But then I felt something touching my fingertips before my hand was even near the tree. I pulled back, rubbing my fingers together. It felt like I had touched water, but my finger was dry. I pointed my flashlight over to the tree again, but the bug was gone. I reached out to touch the tree, feeling the same sensation on all my fingertips.

"Hello!" Rita shouted from directly behind me, startling me, causing me to fall to the ground.

Four

I rolled down a hill, feeling stones and sticks knocking against my body until I finally hit something hard. I kept my eyes squeezed shut, hoping that the fall had truly stopped. I peeked, finding myself under a thick tree. I stayed put for a moment, waiting for my head to stop spinning and for my vision to return to normal. I rubbed my face, hoping not to find something that shouldn't be there. I examined my arms before rising, checking the rest of my body and brushing dirt and leaves from my clothes.

"I'm okay," I shouted. I looked behind me, up the hill I must have tumbled down. I crawled over to my flashlight, took hold of it, and shone it around. I looked up at the tree that had stopped me. It was leaning over oddly, like it was frozen in time. The same green glowing bugs were everywhere now, in the air and on the ground.

One suddenly appeared right in front of me, revealing a little flying insect, just like the one I had seen on the tree. The green light faded. I stood up, looking back at the leaning tree. I had never seen a tree so large before. It was strange, the way it seemed to hang there.

"Rita!" I shouted. "You have to see this." I pointed the flashlight at the hill, hoping Rita would notice the steep incline before falling as I had.

"Rita!" I called again. Something hard hit my foot and knocked me off balance. "Where's my shoes?" I searched for my sandles but didn't see them. "Rita!" I walked over to the hill again. "Rita, I could use your help, or you can just come down here. Just be careful."

I waited for a response, but I heard nothing. I reached into my pockets for the camera that was still there, but the doll was gone.

"Great." I made my way back up the hill, seeing if my shoes and the doll had gotten caught on something.

"Rita!" I yelled louder; but still, she said nothing.

"This isn't funny," I said, making my way back up. I had to stop twice to catch my breath before I finally reached the top. My flashlight must have taken a beating because the light dimmed before it turned completely off. I shouted for Rita again, but there was still nothing. I pulled her camera from my pocket and, shocked, saw it wasn't broken at all. I looked for the option to turn on its flashlight. It seemed much darker out than before. I didn't know if it was tumbling down the hill or the fact that Rita wasn't responding to me that had kept me from noticing the sky before. But finally, I looked up.

There wasn't a deep, dark red sky thickened with clouds anymore. In its place was silver-like glitter spread against a black canvas. I rubbed my fingers against my eyes, then looked back up, blinking a few times, but the atmosphere remained the same. I was frozen, but my eyes rapidly moved across the sky. My body finally shifted to see everything from behind. The sky felt massive. There were billions on top of billions of tiny lights that stretched from one end of the sky to the other. A small wind caressed my neck, reminding me that what I saw was real. My thoughts and voice could only be silenced by the majesty of the alien world. The moon, which was like a stranger now was so clear. Was this our moon? The dark patches that covered it felt foreign. I mean, there were times the moon would be visible in Eradeem, but never like this. I slowly turned to see it all. The sparkles in the sky seemed endless.

"Stars?" The word made its way out of me. I was still trying to understand what I was seeing. I closed my eyes, rubbing my fingers over them. When I opened them, the glitter was still there. *What happened to the sky?* I thought. I looked back at the hill, thinking about how far I must have fallen.

I could see the large tree that I had landed on hanging by its roots. I wondered, suddenly, if maybe I was dead. Could a fall like that kill someone? My heart raced thinking about it. I thought of my parents searching for my body, and Grandpa having to hear the news of my death from a guard. What would Rita do? Would people blame her? I took hold of my chest, trying to calm down, taking in a deep breath. Another cool breeze crested my neck as I closed my eyes.

"I'm okay," I told myself. Billions of stars from a foreign sky were with me. If this was death, it wasn't so bad.

The trees seemed fuller than before, and those green glowing bugs were everywhere. There were sounds I had never heard and the air felt easy to breathe.

I walked in the direction I thought I had come from, calling for Rita again and again. I picked up speed, trying my best to find the open field where the base was. I kept telling myself that I was almost there. I hadn't been in the woods very long at all before the fall, but this was taking forever. It felt like I was just going in circles, completely lost. There was no way to retrace my steps back to the hill so I could start over and get to the field.

The flying lampshades weren't in the sky anymore. I shined the camera's light around, but everything looked the same. I couldn't tell where I had come from. My heart felt like it was ready to beat out of my chest. It was just me, the woods, and the alien sky.

I dropped to my knees, staring at the sky, hoping Rita was okay at least.

"I need help!" I yelled into the darkness. "Help me," I yelled louder and louder until I was screaming.

I threw my palms to the ground, squeezing the dirt, rocks, and grass. "You just have to wake up, Mae," I wept.

Then, a sound grabbed my attention. It was a voice. I wasn't the only one in the forest. I got so quiet; I was holding my breath. Then I heard something from a different direction, in a bush from behind me. It made a strange sound, almost like a baby's cry. I jumped to my feet, and slowly tried to cover the light of the camera, hoping it didn't notice me. I took a deep, dry swallow as I stepped back. I turned around to run, but I immediately smacked into something and hit the ground.

The voice was right above me now, and all I could do was scream and fight the air. "I want to go home!" I had expected to be grabbed, but nothing happened.

"I'm not going to hurt anyone; just calm down, and please stop shining that light in my face," the voice said.

My eyes were squeezed shut; my hands were up for protection, as if that would make the person vanish.

Five

"Are you okay?" the person said, kneeling down to me. I slowly opened my eyes and lowered my hands to see a young man standing before me. It was so dark, but I could see him a little.

"Yeah, yes," I said, giving a nervous smile.

"What are you doing out in the wilderness like this, huh? Are you alone?"

"Yes, I'm lost."

"Okay, well, you're safe now. I can help you get back home. Where are you from?" He reached for my hand. I paused before taking it, but I felt as if I had no choice. I grabbed his hand, and he pulled me to my feet.

"My house is that way," I said, pointing behind me. "I think. I don't know. Maybe if you could help me get to the hill I fell from, that could help me."

"Sure," he said, looking behind him. "There's only one steep hill around here, so that must be what you're talking about? But give me a second." He walked past me and shouted, "Able!" and then made a clicking sound. A small white animal leaped out of the bushes. It galloped towards us and jumped into the man's arms. I fell to the ground in shock.

"What the heck is that!" I screamed.

The young man laughed at my shaking hand, which pointed at the creature.

"It's Abel; he's just a baby. No need to be afraid. Sheep are harmless." He pulled me back to my feet and walked off. "Let's get you back home."

It wasn't very long before we were back at the hilltop, and I explained to him what had happened.

"I'm pretty sure there's nothing in that direction other than woods and desert. Are you sure that's where you fell?"

"Desert?" I said, looking behind me and trying to understand where I was exactly. "No. The desert would be over there." I pointed behind him where the hilltop was.

He looked towards the hill with confusion. "No, Duban City's that way. The closest house I know of is an hour's walk from here."

"I only live fifteen or twenty minutes away, maybe five minutes from my grandfather's base. There's a large grassy field that should be over there somewhere." I pointed in a few directions.

"And where are you from exactly?" the man asked, walking to the other side to get a better look at me.

"Um…well, Meadowed Hills. It's about a forty-minute drive from the city."

"Duban City?" the young man said, scratching his head.

"No!" I answered, taking a hard step away from him.

"And what is your name?"

"My name is Mae."

"Okay. Mae, I am just trying to help you. I've been all through these woods; it's about an hour's walk before you can get out in the direction you're talking about. Then there's just desert."

"Okay, you are really frustrating me. I have never heard of Duban City before. Just point me to where the border is, and I can find my way back from there."

"Border?" He chuckled. "You mean Eradeem's border?"

"What other border would I be talking about?" I said, crossing my arms.

The man scratched his head again, and then stood, frozen, staring off.

"It can't be," he said, looking back at me.

"What?"

"Are you saying that you came from Eradeem?"

"Came from?" I chuckled. But he wasn't laughing back. "What do you mean I came from Eradeem? This is Eradeem."

The man only stared at me, saying nothing.

"Okay, so if this isn't Eradeem, then where am I?"

"You're miles and miles away from Eradeem," the man said.

I wanted to say something, but my words got stuck in my throat. I searched my surroundings, thinking the fall from that hill must have done some damage.

"So, I'm either dead or I'm dreaming right now," I said out loud. "And this man isn't even real. Great."

"Are you okay?" the man said, interrupting me. "I'm pretty sure you aren't dreaming."

"Oh really? I'm not dreaming?" I said, fidgeting my hands, trying to figure out what to do with them. "Then explain that!" I yelled, pointing at the sky.

The man looked up.

"I'm not sure what you are pointing at."

"Hello," I said, dropping my hands. "The sky and… and… and the stars!"

He gave me a blank stare, dropped the baby sheep to the ground, and burst out laughing. All I felt were my emotions desperately trying to escape from me. My chin quivered, and I turned and walked away from the hilltop. I wanted to just run. The last thing I needed was to be laughed at. I could be in danger—or, worse, dead, and this was the afterlife.

"Hey, where are you going?" the man shouted after me. "Please don't leave."

I only stopped because I didn't know where I was going or what I was doing.

"You don't understand," the man shouted.

I turned to look back at him as he walked to me. He stepped into a spot where the moonlight shone through the opening of the woods, revealing him. His black wavy hair hung above his eyes. He wore dark slacks with a sleeveless gray jacket and a white hooded scarf over his shoulders. His eyes were wide as he looked at me with gentleness. It was as if he had found something he had been looking for.

"I didn't mean to scare you. It's just that I haven't met anyone from Eradeem in a long time. I've prayed for this."

"What do you mean?" I asked, feeling a bit more comfortable now that I could see him.

"I've been praying for this moment for a very, very long time. To meet someone from Eradeem. Meeting you here is no accident; this is a miracle."

"Wha…" I shook my head, trying to think and speak at the same time. "What are you talking about?"

He smiled, taking hold of his sheep, which had been behind him. "Come with me, and I will show you." The man took off down the hill. I could either turn back and continue trying to find my way out or follow this stranger to who knows where. I figured that if this was just a dream, what did I have to lose?

"Are you coming?" he called.

———

"I didn't tell you my name," the man said, turning to me when I met him at the bottom of the hill. "I'm Lev." He bowed. I walked past him, avoiding eye contact, but then I stopped myself. I was really irritated at this man, but I felt guilty and didn't want my actions to make me seem ungrateful.

"Nice to meet you," I said, peeking up at him. All I wanted was to be back at home. But Lev's face lit up like a child's; even in the dark, I could see it.

We were at the edge of an open field that stretched farther than I could see. It was populated by more of the white, fluffy animals. They made the same sound as the baby sheep when they saw us approaching, and gathered around us.

The moonlight unveiled how beautiful the land was. The grass, the air, and even the smell was different here.

"What's wrong?" Lev asked, following my gaze to the sky.

"You can't even count how many stars there are, there are so many."

"Yeah." He took in a breath. "It really is incredible."

"So…" I started. I looked over at Lev as I cupped my arms and tugged at my sleeve. "Are those actual stars?"

"Yeah. They are. Have you never seen a star before?"

I was here because I was trying to find out what had happened to Grandpa, and somehow his life's work was staring down at me. Satisfaction washed over me as I watched the sky. Even though he was in jail for it, it felt like it wasn't for nothing. I wiped the tear from the corner of my eye.

"Eradeem must be a very strange place now," Lev said, breaking my fixation on the vastness of the sky.

"Why is that?"

"It seems like this is the first time you are seeing them?"

"We rarely see the moon, but the sky here is so clear. In Eradeem, people don't really know what a star is. It's considered a myth. My grandpa, though…. He's been trying to prove they exist ever since I could remember." I paused. "He was arrested today."

"Why?" Lev asked.

"I don't know. That's why I'm out here. I thought that maybe it was because of his research on stars."

"Hmm, there are a lot of lost people in Eradeem then. Your grandfather sounds like a very brave man."

"I guess he is." I added, "So, these are all sheep?"

"Yes, and I am their shepherd."

"Oh," I said. "What's a shepherd?"

"Well, someone who looks after sheep."

"Why do you have to look after them?"

"Because sheep are pretty dumb. They need a shepherd to lead them or they will get lost, just like the one I found up the hill with you. In exchange, I sell their wool for money, and I make a living that way."

"Wool?"

"The white stuff on their back." He chuckled. "You know, that's how clothes are made."

"What?" I asked, touching my shirt.

Lev chuckled again. "I bet you don't know where your food comes from either?"

"It's created in the factories."

"More like it's processed in the factories. Your food comes from out here. I'm pretty sure the plants and animals you eat are one hundred percent not from Eradeem."

I didn't respond; I wasn't sure what to say to that. I was already overwhelmed enough.

"So, I'm curious," Lev said, turning to me. "Do you know how you got here?"

"I'm pretty sure I bumped my head when I fell down the hill. This is probably just a dream, or something worse."

"Worse?"

"Yeah, or—I'm dead." I didn't want to say that part.

"Well, if you're dead, does that make me God, then?"

My eyes widened. The thought of God had never occurred to me.

He laughed. "I promise that you aren't dead. Do you remember what you were doing before you bumped your head?"

"I was with my friend Rita. We were at my grandpa's base trying to figure out what he had been up to. Then we saw these floating lampshade things in the sky, and I followed them, trying to see where they were coming from. Then I saw those green light bugs," I said, pointing to the field, which was covered with glowing green lights. "Before I knew it, I was falling. I came back up the hill, and the sky was different, and Rita was gone."

"You have a good memory for someone who bumped their head." He smirked. "Floating lampshades?" He rubbed his chin, looking up into the sky. "You must mean the lanterns?"

"Lanterns?"

"Yeah, you light them with fire, and they float away with the wind."

He walked over to one of them sitting by a tree. He handed it to me, grinning. "It's not a lampshade, but they kind of look like it. They're sent out every night just for Eradeem, in hopes that someone will see them. And maybe that someone will get curious and try to find out where they're coming from. Maybe even come this far," Lev said, glancing over at me.

"Well, I'm telling you that it wasn't a long distance. I don't live far from here."

"Let me show you something." He walked, making a clicking sound as he moved among the sheep. They all got up and followed him. Holding the lantern in one hand, I reached out with the other, feeling the gentleness of their soft wool. There were about twenty of them, including a couple of babies. We walked up a steep hill until we reached the highest point in the area. There below us was the forest. Lev stretched his hand out, pointing past it.

"It's difficult to see because we're so far, but do you notice that red glow?" I looked at where he was pointing.

"I think so," I said, squinting. The land was foggy from a distance, but I could see a red glow stretched over the middle of the horizon.

"That's Eradeem," Lev said.

"That's Eradeem?" I chuckled. "So, are you telling me I crossed a desert? That's proof I'm dreaming."

"Yes, that's Eradeem; and, no, you aren't dreaming. I do believe you, Mae, when you say you didn't cross a desert. That's why you being here is a miracle. I've prayed for a very long time that I would get a chance to talk to someone from Eradeem. I hoped someone in that city would follow the lanterns. And look, you are here, flesh and blood before me."

"So, *you* made these lanterns in hopes someone would follow them?"

"No, I don't make them. A very good friend of mine does." He paused, looking away from me. He blinked a few times and smirked. "Actually, we are more than just good friends. But it worked. You're here. It took a long time."

I walked closer to the edge of the cliff, looking at Eradeem.

"So, right now…" I started, trying to grasp what he was telling me. "I am beyond the border." I turned to look at him. "Eradeem's border."

He nodded once.

"I'm on the outside of Eradeem, right?"

"Correct."

"Then why does everything seem so… not bad? I thought everything was toxic out here. No one could survive living outside of Eradeem."

"It seems like stars aren't the only thing about the world Eradeem didn't teach you. I assure you that the desert isn't toxic. Hostile, but not toxic."

"If you wanted to meet people in Eradeem, why haven't you crossed the desert to go yourself?"

"I can't." Lev walked over to a fire pit made of large stones. He grabbed some wood nearby, bringing it to the pit and away from the cliff. "Outsiders aren't allowed to enter Eradeem."

"Why not?"

"Because that's Eradeem's law. You aren't allowed past the border, and I am not allowed to cross the desert. I'm guessing your next question is why? Because they don't want you or anyone living in Eradeem to know the truth."

"What truth?"

"That Eradeem is nothing more than a prison."

"Eradeem isn't a prison," I said, following Lev. The sheep came along and settled around the pit.

"What is a prison, Mae?" Lev asked me.

"It's…" I started, thinking maybe this was a trick question. "It's … a place you go if you committed a crime."

"And?"

"And you are locked away from the world."

"Yes, a prison is a place that locks one away from the outside world, with no freedom. You have no idea what is going on outside of the walls of Eradeem. Simply being out here for the first time and seeing stars shocks you. Why? Because you have been a prisoner of Eradeem since birth, just like everyone else there. I've prayed I could just reach one person in Eradeem to tell them the truth." Lev continued taking the wood to the pit.

"Why just one?" I asked.

"One person is all it takes," he said, tossing the wood and dry grass onto the pit. He pulled out two black squares and rubbed them together until a spark jumped from them and into the dry grass, causing a small fire.

"Well, this is the weirdest dream I have ever had," I said, walking over to get a better look as Lev cupped his hands around the small flames and blew at them. The glow of the flames slowly grew, lighting up the night. Although it wasn't very cold out, the warmth was comforting.

"Maybe you're right and this is just a dream; but if that is the case, when you wake up, remember what I am about to tell you," Lev said, standing.

"What's with the fire?"

"A story is always better when there is a nice fire going. Don't you think?"

"So, you're going to tell me a story?"

"I'm going to tell you your history." Lev sat on the ground against a stone, signaling me to join him. I sat across from him, taking a seat on another stone nearby. The fire's glow revealed how handsome he was. He had narrow, kind eyes and an olive complexion, much lighter than mine, covered in stubble. He looked to be in his early twenties. The more I looked at him, though, I noticed how strange his appearance was. His skin was so clear. It was difficult to see any hint of a mask covering the Abnormal. It was like he wasn't wearing a mask at all.

"So, how much money do shepherds make exactly?"

"Depends on how many sheep they have, and how hard they work."

"So, are these considered a lot of sheep?" I asked.

Lev chuckled. "Not at all. I have friends with hundreds of them. But my pay is decent, and I also lend a hand to other farmers from time to time."

"Do they pay well?" I asked. Lev only chuckled.

"Why do you keep asking about my pay? Do I look like a poor man to you?"

"No, no," I replied, waving my hands. "Sorry if I'm being rude. It's just that the kind of mask you're wearing, usually only rich people can afford that. Not to say you're poor. I was just curious. It's really hard to see it.

"A mask? What do you mean?"

"Well…" I looked away as I started. "I can always see when someone is wearing one. Unless they're rich and have gotten surgery done, or can afford a Fadota mask."

Lev only stared at me. "I've never heard of Fadota. I'm guessing mask is an Eradeem thing, then. No one wears any kind of mask out here."

"Really?" I said, scratching my head. "So, what do you do about

Abnormal?"

"Abnormal?" he repeated, lifting an eyebrow. "I don't think I've ever heard of Abnormal. I mean, something being abnormal, yes, or…ooh!" he said, slapping his knee and laughing.

"What's so funny?" I ask.

"Are you talking about the curse?"

"Uh, I don't know?"

"The mark everyone's born with on the chest."

"Well, sort of."

"It eventually spreads all over your body as vine-like, scaly rashes. Is that what you mean by Abnormal?"

"Yes?"

"Nope, I got none of that." He lifted his shirt and patted his chest. "Nothing here."

"What?" I said, leaning forward and squinting. "Huh, I guess you don't."

"You don't believe me, do you?"

"I mean, people do get surgeries, but you don't seem rich."

He walked over to me and kneeled to my eye level. He reached for my hand with a smile. "I'm not going to hurt you, Mae," he said. He took my hand, placing it on his cheek, forehead, and chin. His skin was so soft. He had a freckle or two, but there was nothing else: no mask or any signs of Abnormal.

"Believe me now? Feels just like yours. This is all me. One hundred percent all-natural."

"How is that possible?" I asked. Lev went back to his seat. I pulled my collar down a bit to take a peek at the little spot that sat over my heart. It was still there.

Lev's smile slowly fell as he stared into the fire, poking it with a twig. "What you call Abnormal, out here is called 'the curse.' And it isn't normal, Mae. I don't know how bad things have gotten in Eradeem, but I can only imagine. Eradeem has been keeping a secret from you, from everyone living in that city."

"A secret?"

"That everything you have ever known is a lie," Lev said, staring over at me. I didn't want him to go any further, but I couldn't help but listen.

"Something inside of you has always known that, hasn't it?" Lev continued. "You've always known something wasn't right your whole life, haven't you? Everyone in Eradeem feels the same way, Mae. But there's something about you that is making it hard to accept. The only difference between people in Eradeem and those living beyond the border is that the curse doesn't reign here. Most people here only have the mark over the chest, as I'm sure you have, and some are totally clear, just as I am. But the curse in Eradeem is deeply rooted and slowly changing people into the unimaginable."

"What do you mean by 'the unimaginable?' "

"Creatures," Lev responded.

I was silent, trembling slightly. My mind wanted to reject what he was saying, but something inside me believed him. I'd heard stories of creatures roaming the neighborhood, but I'd thought they were just urban legends. Stories of monsters suddenly appearing in people's homes, or out on the street. I had never known anyone personally who became a creature. Only that someone knew someone it happened to. Even though it seemed crazy, for the first time, it also felt right, like something I had known three years ago and had repressed.

Six

"Eradeem was originally called the City of Light," Lev started. "I don't know what it's like to live in Eradeem now, but the City of Light could be compared to how things are out here. The curse, or the Abnormal as you call it, didn't really exist at that time like it does now. Back then, the curse was something you chose, not something you were just born with."

"Why would someone choose to have a curse?" I asked, leaning in.

"I know it sounds crazy now, but the curse granted extraordinary power. A power not allowed in Light."

"Power… You mean like magic powers?"

"Yes. The power to control and influence. Light wasn't a perfect place, but it was as close to heaven as you could get. There were no grandfathers arrested for unreasonable crimes or technology that polluted the sky, causing strange clouds. People were extremely generous, whether they had a lot or a little. They rarely felt they were lower or higher than anyone. They appreciated the differences in each other, and they had respect for one another. They even had a king."

"A king? Eradeem had a king?" I interrupted.

"A whole court. It was a peaceful time." Lev paused, then looked up at the sky. "But the most important person in the City of Light was the counselor." He stared down at the flames and pushed a log closer to the fire with a stick.

"What was so important about a counselor?"

"He was immortal," Lev said, looking back at me as if waiting for a reaction.

"Okay." I laughed. But he didn't react back.

"They were close friends, the king and counselor. They both spent a lot of their time with the people in Light. Light wasn't a small place, yet the king and counselor knew almost everyone by name. The counselor helped guide the king in ruling Light, and the king trusted everything the counselor said. They created a culture where people would always have the opportunity to choose righteousness. Anyone who couldn't work was taken care of. It was a time when the community cared for the weak. The best part was that not only did the king have access to the counselor, but so did everyone who lived in Light. The curse granted extraordinary power—but so did the counselor. He wanted everyone to have access to him so they didn't have to choose a curse."

"Huh, so an immortal friend who never dies grants anyone who knows him power? Nope, that doesn't sound like something someone made up at all."

"It sounds that crazy, huh?" Lev replied, keeping his smile and gentle eyes on me. "Guess for anyone who lives in Eradeem, that probably sounds like a myth."

"Yeah, but I am enjoying your story." I smiled, eager to hear more.

"It sounds strange, but that kind of stuff was normal. The palace sat on the very edge of Light on a hill." He pointed back to Eradeem. "There used to be a large sea that separated Light from other far-off lands. The desert that separates Eradeem from where we are now used to be that sea." I straightened up and looked over to the desert.

"So, what happened to the sea?" I replied, tucking my arms around my belly, imagining a body of water there. Lev's story was ridiculous, but something about the sea turning into a desert felt true.

"It dried up after the curse spread," Lev replied "Ever since then, it's never been the same."

"So, then, why did the curse spread?"

"Now you are asking the right question. It began when the king fell in love with an outsider. Her name was Premleen."

"A love story? This just got more interesting."

Lev leaned back against a stone and continued. "She was a master of poisons and medicines. Because of her techniques, people feared her," Lev said as his face became serious. "People could only see Premleen as dangerous, even when she proved herself to be good. She was accused of being a witch, so she lived her days alone, making money by selling medicine to those who would buy it.

But one day, she was called to the palace. The king was seriously sick, and only Premleen had the cure for him. During the treatment, she was the only one allowed to care for him. They quickly became friends; then, more slowly, they fell in love.

"The king proudly confessed his love to her in front of all of Light, and, shortly after, they were engaged. People believed she put a spell on the king, but that wasn't true. As time passed, more people started to see her the way the king did, as someone good. But then all that was undone." Lev paused again, looking back at the fire. He pressed his lips together, taking in a slow breath.

"Premleen found herself lost in the woods one day," he continued. "She ran into a man claiming to be an old friend of the king's. The stranger filled Premleen's head with lies about him and the City of Light. Premleen didn't believe the stranger at first; but, because of her compassion, she kept visiting him, and slowly she grew to believe his lies. Her heart became hardened toward the king."

"If she was so in love with the king, how could she believe a stranger over him?" I asked.

"He had convinced Premleen that they were the same. They were both outsiders, feared by people and abandoned by society. He told her that he was banished to the woods by the king for a simple misunderstanding. He convinced her that in the same way she used odd plants and poisons to find cures for sickness, he was using the power of the curses to do good, but people didn't understand. He told her that she was the only person who understood him; and if the king knew they were talking, she could no longer see him. Premleen understood what it was like to be alone and abandoned. She knew what it was like to be misunderstood.

"So, she visited him daily. The counselor knew what was going on with Premleen and warned the king of her involvement with the stranger. The king assured the counselor that regardless of whom Premleen was talking to, he trusted her and believed that she could never betray him. The counselor pleaded with the king to stop the relationship between the stranger and Premleen, but the king wanted Premleen to have the freedom to decide who he was on her own.

"Then one day, after the stranger gained Premleen's total trust, he asked for a favor. He wanted to give the king a gift, and he wanted her to deliver it on his behalf. He told her that this gift could restore his broken relationship with the king. That this was the way for the king to finally forgive him. Premleen wanted to help so badly and agreed. He handed Premleen an elaborate, carved stone container, telling her that only the king could open it.

"As she made her way back to the city with the gift from the stranger, she was stopped by the counselor. The counselor had been watching Premleen and warned her that the gift would kill her lover. But the stranger had warned Premleen about the counselor, saying that he was not to be trusted. So, she didn't listen to him.

"Once she arrived at the palace, she found the king and brought the gift from the stranger. When the King opened the container, a curse was released. The king dropped it, cracking the container, and a thick vine appeared from the ground, engulfing him in a cocoon. The vines filled the palace, destroying everyone and everything in their way. Then the effects of the curse began spreading in the city. The curse didn't slowly appear as you become older, like now. The worst of the curse plagued everyone, even children. The most terrible part was that the children of the city died because their bodies couldn't handle it. The cries of the people echoed throughout the city as their children died in their arms. Every single person became covered with an unsightly abnormality.

"But poor Premleen got the worst of it. The curse turned her into a beast. Scales for skin, claws for hands and feet. A long tail and a large head. And in the middle of the chaos, the stranger entered the City of Light, announcing to the people that the king was dead. He pinned Premleen as the murderer and the cause of the curse, and told the people that the only way to stop the curse was for everyone to put their trust in him. The stranger revealed his power by healing a dead child in his mother's arms. Without a second thought, the people rushed to him to be cured. One by one, he cleared the sickness from every person and brought every child back to life, only leaving a mark on every person's chest.

"Premleen was afraid of what might happen to her. So, she escaped into the wilderness alone. The only one not affected by the catastrophe was the counselor. The counselor made his way into the vine-covered palace and found that the king was still alive among the vines. The counselor was able to release him, taking the king's weak body to the back of the palace, where the sea was. The counselor found a small sail boat and used it to take himself and the king away. The farther from the City of Light they went, the more the king's strength returned. All he could think about was Premleen.

"He demanded that the counselor return him to Light to find her. The counselor warned the king that if he returned, he would die; but the king still insisted on finding her. So, the counselor turned the boat around and headed for the woods. The king understood that of all of those in Eradeem with the curse, the strongest came from Premleen. The closer he got to her, the weaker he would become. When they reached land, the king could barely stand, but he kept going. He could feel exactly where she was and followed where his weakness led.

"He could hear Premleen's cries echoing throughout the woods as he pushed through the forest, trying not to lose his footing. Each time he collapsed, he pushed himself up to continue. When he finally found her, she was unrecognizable. She was near the cave where the stranger had lived, hunched over a large stone.

"The closer he got to her, the colder the king began to feel, and the slower his breathing became. The king called out to Premleen. When she heard his voice, she raised her head slowly. She watched him drag his body in her direction. Her eyes widened, believing that she was seeing a ghost, and he saw the fear in her eyes.

"'No...no,' Premleen cried, quickly hiding her face as the king approached her.

"The king fell to his hands and knees before her, calling out her name. Pushing his body back up to stand, he moved closer to Premleen, reaching out to touch her black, scaly face and lifting her head to see him.

"She said, 'I'm so sorry,' as her tears soaked the king's hands. The king used all his strength to pull Premleen into his arms, holding her tight.

"'Nothing can stop me from loving you, Premleen.'" Those were his last words before he died."

"He died?" I interrupted, and Lev nodded.

"As his lifeless body lay in her arms, all she could feel was shame. She pulled his body against hers, not realizing her hands and body had returned to normal. His love had cured the curse.

"Unlike the people in Light, who appeared to be free from the curse with only the mark on their chest, Premleen was completely cured, with no mark at all. The stranger became the new immortal ruler, changing Light into Eradeem. The sea dried up, and an invisible barrier trapped the people of Eradeem for generations."

I remained silent when he finished. Lev stared off to the desert.

"You're a really good storyteller. I would have thought you where there, witnessing everything. You really love Eradeem," I said.

He looked down, smiling.

"So, the king died because of her?"

"He did. Although the curse didn't affect the king like everyone else, it was still toxic to the king. The only way to survive was to leave Light forever, but his love for Premleen took his life," Lev said.

"That is the history of the Abnormal?"

"Yes, that is the history," Lev said, smiling.

"It reminds me of a book back at my grandpa's base."

"Really? What book is that?"

"I don't know. I can't read it, but it's a picture book for kids. I can't really remember all of it. But it's like what you're saying. My grandpa was reading it before he was taken."

"Well, maybe it's a sign?"

"A sign of what?"

"That what I'm telling you is true."

"That's a kid's book."

"So?"

"It's for kids, so it's some kind of fairy tale, just like your story sounds like a fairy tale."

"Well, my dear, it is the truth." Lev tilted his head slightly, looking past me and smiling. "You know, they say even though the counselor is no longer here, he can appear as a cardinal." I followed his gaze to a red bird in the tree above my head.

"Weird," I said. "Seems like this bird keeps following me."

"It's probably because you're special, Mae. It's not every day someone can bypass the barrier that traps people inside Eradeem. That's not a small thing."

"Barrier," I said, chuckling. "You expect me to believe that?"

"Well, I hope you would, but I can definitely see why you wouldn't."

"I'm sorry to break it to you, but no one would ever believe this story in Eradeem. It's very clear that you really believe it, though, so maybe there is some truth to it."

"It's that crazy, huh?"

I shrugged. "My grandfather is a famous scientist, and people think he's a freak for even trying to prove the existence of stars. So, I think you have a long way to go to get anyone to think that Abnormal is some curse. You're just a man living in the woods."

"Well, Mae Meadows," Lev said as he stood. I rose as he approached me. "Regardless of whether you believe my story, please don't forget it. It was a pleasure meeting you."

"I don't remember telling you my last name," I stated.

"Is it really that strange that I know your last name if this is just a dream?" Lev said, smiling and reaching out his hand for me to shake.

"I guess you're right," I replied, taking his hand. It was warm.

"Well, this is goodbye." His palm began to heat up, and a slow breeze caused Lev's hair to dance. "It was a pleasure meeting you."

He smiled as the wind picked up more until there was a gust all around us. I looked over at the flames as they grew higher, unaffected by the wind. "I will see you again, Mae," Lev said. I started to feel the warmth from his hand moving up my arm to my shoulder. Then the sensation was moving throughout my body as the wind seemed to circulate around us, blowing through my hair and clothes. Lev stopped shaking my hand and only held it. My eyes widened as my body became warmer and warmer.

"What's happening?" I yelled over the sound of the wind.

Light started coming from him. It got brighter and brighter until I had to close my eyes. Then everything stopped. The wind stopped, the warmth stopped, and I could no longer feel Lev's hand.

I opened my eyes, expecting to see trees and Lev right in front of me; but all I saw was my bedroom wall with the clock over my door reading 8:23. I rose from my bed and looked out the window, not sure if it was morning or evening. I threw the covers off, my feet reaching for the floor. I was fully dressed in the same clothes.

I stood in that same place for a while, trying to figure out what had happened. Did I even go to Grandpa's base last night? Maybe I took a nap, forgetting to leave for the base. As crazy as the dream was, it felt more real than any dream I'd ever had. I was almost afraid to leave my bedroom. Walking over to the door, I cracked it open, peeking out, but I couldn't hear anything. I wondered if the fall from the hill had left me unconscious, and my parents had found me outside and brought me back.

That thought was so terrifying that I knew that had to be it. If that was the case, I was in big trouble, but hiding in my room wasn't going to change anything. If I got hurt out there, it was obvious my parents knew I was out past curfew. I touched around my head for any bumps as I tried to come up with an excuse; but then I remembered Rita had probably told my parents everything. There was no hiding, so I took a deep breath and opened the door.

"Mom," I called out. "Dad?" I walked from my room to the staircase, peeking down, but I saw and heard nothing. My parents' bedroom door was open. I glanced inside, but no one was there, just their unmade bed. I walked to their window to see if their car was still there, and everything was as it had been last night. The sound of the front door opening brought my attention downstairs. Footsteps came from the stairs as I made my way back into the hall. Rita appeared. I was a little relieved. I figured the first wave of anger from her would get me ready for my parents.

"Mae?" Rita said, looking puzzled as she stepped into the hall. "You're okay!" she shouted, running to embrace me. "I thought something bad happened to you."

"I'm sure I just hit my head," I said, hugging Rita back.

"Where were you? Did you get lost or something? Everyone is out looking for you. We had to call the Vigilant and everything."

"You called the Vigilant?" I asked.

"We had to; you've been gone for hours, Mae. I need to go tell everyone you're home." She ran toward the stairs.

"Rita!" I shouted. "What are you talking about? I woke up in my bed."

"What?"

"I thought you found me out in the woods and had my parents come and get me."

"I was just with your parents; they're still out looking for you. What are you talking about?"

"I fell down the hill in the woods. You were the one who knocked me over," I cried.

"Yeah, I thought I saw you, but then you were gone."

"Then who brought me back home? I just woke up in bed, not even five minutes ago."

"Ah," Rita said, giving a nervous laugh. "Let me go get your parents." Rita took off down the stairs and I followed behind.. "Ms. Meadows," she called. "I found Mae."

My mother appeared around the corner of the porch, the phone to her ear.

"Oh my God. Honey, Rita found her." My mother walked over, taking me in her arms. "Where were you?" she cried.

"She was in the house," Rita responded.

"What?" My mother looked at Rita, then back to me.

"I've been here the whole time," Mom said. "I stayed just in case you came back."

"No!" I said, pulling back from my mother. "I woke up in my room. Someone brought me there."

"What?" My mom furrowed her brow. "Who? I've been here the whole time. What were you even doing outside past curfew in the first place?"

"I..." I started, but then I realized what the real issue was. I was doing what I knew I wasn't supposed to be doing.

"I just wanted to go to Grandpa's base."

"Really. So, you couldn't do that earlier in the day, or wait till morning? You had to go right then, in the dark?" Mom said with her arms crossed. "You expect me to believe that, and that someone just brought you home, too?"

"But Mom…"

"Go to your room, and I will deal with you later," Mom demanded. "I need to let the Vigilant know you're back."

Seven

I didn't talk to Rita until I returned to school two days later. Because of her high grades, she was in more advanced classes than I was, so I had to wait until the assembly at the end of the day to see her. Rita was supposed to present her project in front of the whole school for the chance to be chosen as a student at Lukenic for the next academic year.

Students were still arriving when I entered the auditorium. Kids clustered together in their cliques hoping to sit together, while the rest of us tried to find any free seat. I knew I would be sitting alone, since Rita would be presenting.

Seven students sat on the stage waiting patiently for the program to start. I searched for Rita among them, but she was nowhere to be found. I looked around the room, thinking she was just late. Perhaps she was doing something important, or maybe her nerves had gotten to her. Maybe she was just backstage collecting herself.

But as I looked for a place to sit among my classmates, I spotted Rita's usual soft-pink hair clip. She sat in the middle seat of the auditorium, alone.

"What are you doing here?" I said, approaching from behind. My heart sank to my belly at the look she gave me. Had I done something wrong? I sat down next to her, feeling guilty. Was it possible that she wasn't onstage because of me?

"Is everything okay?" I asked. Rita's eyes were bloodshot.

She looked away from me and exhaled.

"I didn't finish my project."

"But…" I paused for a second. "I thought my dad was helping you and…"

"No, Mae. I planned to finish after going home and then practice my speech; but after you went missing that night, my parents found out that I was in the woods with you past curfew. They spent that whole day yelling at me. I couldn't focus the whole weekend. I stayed up until two a.m. last night, and I got nowhere. Then when I came in this morning to present what I had, they told me I was disqualified because I broke curfew with you."

"Are you serious?"

She didn't respond. My hands balled up on my lap as I looked away. I was so confused about what had happened that night, I hadn't thought about the trouble I'd gotten her in.

"Rita?" I glanced at her. "I'm so sorry."

"It's okay," Rita said, keeping her gaze forward. "Now we can go to the same school, just like you wanted."

The lights in the room dimmed. I took a seat next to Rita and the assembly began. Rita narrowed her lips and sniffled, trying to hold in her anger. A man walked to the front of the stage where a podium and microphone sat. I couldn't pay attention to his speech.

I wanted this assembly to end, and quickly. I had spent the last three years listening to Rita talk about Lukenic and prepare for this one day. It was torture to sit next to her as her dreams vanished before her, because of me. I didn't mean for things to go so far. I just wanted to know what my parents were not telling me about Grandpa.

I knew everyone believed I was lying about waking up in bed, but how could I show them that I was telling the truth? I guessed all that didn't matter, anyway, because I had been out past curfew.

"Wow, I can't believe he's here." Rita's voice snapped me back to the assembly. I looked at the stage to see a new man standing there as the whole auditorium stood to clap. I recognized the man, but I wasn't quite sure how.

"Who's that?" I asked, joining the applause.

"Aren't you paying any attention?" Rita glanced over at me. "That's Vich Caven? The Chief Presidential Advisor. He's aided a lot of our leaders." He was an older man with white hair, but he didn't look old enough to be an advisor for many presidents. The last president was in office for twenty years, and this current one had been in office since I was born. He wore an all-black suit with a black collared shirt underneath. He was tall, slim, and must have had the best cosmetic surgery I had ever seen.

As everyone took a seat, he thanked the room, saying he was honored to be at our school to present the awards. He called out a series of students' names, handing each their designated award. But only one of the students was going to be picked to go to Lukenic.

"Why is he at *our* school? It isn't that famous."

"He must be touring around other schools, too," Rita said, holding both hands together, rubbing her thumbnail against her other palm.

The presentation lasted for about an hour. The winner was announced, and we were dismissed to return home. Now what? I thought to myself. Rita didn't leave immediately. She sat with her hands pressed against her lap, looking at the back of the seat in front of her. With everything that had happened, I was surprised she could pay attention to the stage.

"My instructor wants to talk to me," Rita said, as the room began to clear.

"About what?"

"I don't know, he just said to stay behind to see him after the assembly. He told me this after he learned I had been disqualified."

I didn't respond. I wished there was something I could do to fix this, but knew it was too late.

"Maybe he wants to tell me more bad news," Rita said as she noticed her instructor standing near the stage, waving her over. He was talking to the other guests who represented Lukenic. She rose from her seat, letting out a heavy sigh.

"Can I come with you?" I said, stopping her. She paused for a moment, then shrugged.

I followed her and, as we got closer, we realized that the Chief Advisor was with the instructor as well. Rita almost stumbled when she saw him.

"Are you okay?" I asked, coming to her side.

"I'm fine," she said, reassuring herself; but she had turned pale.

Once we were close enough, the instructor acknowledged us by opening the circle of important people.

"This is Rita, the one I was telling you about. She is our top-performing student."

"Miss Rita Manna. I've heard a lot about you," the Advisor said with an emotionless face. He seemed much taller up close. He offered his hand to Rita.

Her jaw dropped as she took it. She looked like she wanted to say something, but no words escaped her lips.

"I was hoping to see the project you would present here today. I'm disappointed that I couldn't."

Rita's eyes widened. I wanted to enter Rita's body and speak for her. She looked humiliated. I couldn't take seeing her the way she was. Her strong, confident, smart personality was gone.

"Wait!" I said, snatching the attention away from Rita. It was as if the circle had just realized I was there.

"It's not Rita's fault she couldn't present. She's the smartest girl I know. If it weren't for me, she would have been on stage today. She was just trying to help me… help me look for stars…." I immediately froze, horrified by what had just come out of my mouth. How could I say that, out of all the things in the world?

"I mean, not that Rita believes in such things." I laughed nervously. Rita eyes stretched wider than I'd ever seen them. She could drop dead right there, and I would be her murderer. The look on everyone's faces proved I'd made things worse.

"I am terribly sorry about this," the instructor said, turning to the Chief Advisor with both hands clutched together like he was begging for forgiveness. "This is in no way a reflection of the education here. I promise you that." He threw a look at me.

"No, it's okay. There's nothing wrong with a little creativity," the Chief Advisor said. He looked at me with a small smile. "And what's your name, young lady?"

I was in trouble. Why did he want to know my name? "Um. It's Mae Meadows, sir."

"Huh…Meadows. You must be related to Niles Cefend, am I right?"

"Y-yes," I said. "He's my grandfather."

"That makes sense. He's the only one I know who speaks of stars.

You must get a lot of your creativity from him. It's something that's missing in society these days."

"You know him?" I asked.

"We've met, but his reputation precedes him."

"Is that a good thing?" I asked as laughter followed from the circle.

"My, you do speak rather bluntly," the Advisor said back. "Your grandfather is a genius. His work in Fadota cosmetics has done wonders in the mask industries, and that's something to be proud of." It took a moment for me to comprehend what he was saying. It didn't seem as if he had a bad opinion of my grandpa, which was a first. It made sense that my grandfather might have met the Chief Advisor in the past, since he used to be a very popular scientist in his younger years. I wondered if the Advisor knew that Grandpa had been arrested.

"Now, back to you, Rita," the Advisor started. "I heard that you have been working very hard to become a student at Lukenic and I wanted to offer my recommendation."

"W-what?" Rita said, looking over at me.

"It would be an immediate acceptance, Rita," the Chief Advisor said.

Rita wobbled back a little, blinking like she didn't believe what she had heard.

I leaned over, whispering to Rita, "This is when you say 'thank you.'"

"Thank you. Thank you so much."

"Your instructor will contact your parents afterward, and I hope that you will enjoy your time at Lukenic, Miss Rita. Congratulations. It was nice to meet you. Oh, and you, too, Mae."

Rita and I slowly turned away from the group of adults, trying to hide our pure excitement.

"I've been accepted into Lukenic," Rita said.

"That's good news. I told you that you didn't need a project to get in. You're super smart, Rita."

Rita stopped walking and turned to me. "What was that about back there? I know you were trying to help, but why did you start talking about stars?"

"I don't know. But I'm glad I mentioned Grandpa."

"It would have been better to mention Grandpa and nothing about stars," Rita replied.

"Well, that didn't make a difference, did it? They already declared you a winner before the day even started."

"Yeah," Rita said.

"I'm sorry that I almost messed things up for you. So, I guess we won't be going to the same school after all."

"No, I'm sorry for being sarcastic about that."

"Right," I said, forcing a smile.

"I better get going. I have to tell my family."

"Wait," I said, stopping her. "I need to talk to you about what happened over the weekend. A part of me didn't want to bring it up, since it almost cost you going to Lukenic; but I really need help understanding what happened that night I disappeared. You were right behind me when I fell, and…"

"Mae," Rita stopped me. "I do need to go. We can talk later, okay?" She took off before I could say anything else.

I decided to take the long way home. I wasn't eager to get there now that Grandpa was gone. I decided to walk to my second bus stop to avoid my parents and any discussion about my disappearance. If I shared with my parents about the man in the woods, I wasn't sure what they would think.

Maybe they would think that I had lost my mind or that I was lying. I remembered everything so clearly, except how I got home. I remembered the man's name was Lev, and that I'd somehow made it hundreds of miles outside of Eradeem. I guessed that was proof right there that it was just a dream. How could someone travel so far in a short amount of time? I tried accepting that it was just a dream, but I struggled because it had all felt so real. Dreams were like that sometimes. The last thing I remembered was Lev saying goodbye.

I hardly noticed how late it was getting until the hissing sound of the streetlamps flickering on with a red glow. Thick blankets of clouds continued their daily blockage of the sun, making it hard to tell when it was night. I paused, looking up, remembering the blackened night that had consumed me and the silver shards in the sky that had pierced my soul. The lights from the city were so strong in Eradeem. A black sky could never take over. Grandpa had mentioned before that total darkness was the best way to see stars. It didn't make sense to me before, but it was starting to now.

Orient sky, ablaze with stellary fire
Sent to guide the flight
Journey through the night
Over mountains and mire

Someone yelled from across the street, a homeless man holding a cardboard sign reading, "The end is near." He paced back and forth on the sidewalk, reciting these words repeatedly to anyone walking by.

Orient sky, ablaze with stellary fire
Sent to guide the flight
Journey through the night
Over mountains and mire

He wore a cardboard mask over his face—two holes for the eyes and an opening for the mouth. A pile of his belonging sat in a cart beside him. I stayed across the street, watching him try to get the attention of the cars that drove by.

Where had I heard that? Why was it so familiar? Then, sticking out of his cart, I saw what looked like the same lanterns from Grandpa's base.

"That can't be," I said, making my way across the street to the cart. The man continued to recite his message. I reached out to take the lantern, then paused, realizing it didn't belong to me.

"Excuse me," I said to the man. "Where did you find this?" I pointed to his cart. It had the same symbol like the lantern at Grandpa's base. He turned to me, lifting his rectangular cardboard mask over his head, and looked me in the eye. His overgrown beard made him appear older than he was. His shoes were falling apart, and he smelled like he hadn't showered in weeks. But I was taken aback by his face, which had no blemish, spot, or vein. There was no Abnormal in sight.

Ghost, bird, man, king
To Eradeem, the light they bring
They alone can bring back peace
Once beast beneath has been unleashed

He was reciting the words from the first lantern I'd found at Grandpa's base.

"Where did you get this?" I pushed.

"Where else?" he said, pointing to the sky. "It's from the outside world."

Eight

"The outside?" I asked as his blue eyes locked with mine. "Someone from the outside is trying to reach us," he said, stepping toward me.

"They want us to know the truth." A woman walking with her child, pulled the kid in closer to her thighs trying to protect him from seeing us, as she turned her head away.

Everyone who had walked past ignored him, and some sneered in disgust at the man because they saw him as unclean, yet he was the one who had no Abnormal. He had something they spent their whole lives trying to achieve.

"Your Abnormal. What hap …" I started, then stopped myself, realizing I was reaching out to him, but the man took my hand and pressed it against his dusty cheek. All I felt was flesh dried out from the sun.

"I woke up one day, and I was cured, he said, smiling ear to ear.

"Cured? what do you mean?"

"We are all cursed, everyone in this forsaken city." His eyes widened and became glossy. "You're young and you still have time. You can't let this city take your essence like it did to me, but somehow, I've been freed. Someone freed me."

"Someone did this to you?" I repeated. But then the man was yanked back suddenly, as a couple of Vigilant appeared from behind, taking hold of him.

"Wait," I shouted. "He did nothing wrong!" I wanted to stop them, but what could I do?

"You're not wearing a mask?" one of them yelled as they put him on the ground.

"Look at his face," I shouted again. "He has no Abnormal."

But they weren't listening. One of the Vigilant threatened to take me because of curfew if I didn't leave. I stepped aside and only watched as they handcuffed and led the man into a vehicle. It wasn't uncommon for the Vigilant to stop someone for not wearing a mask. It was only when someone didn't comply that they would do something about it, but this was the first I'd seen them become so violent over someone not wearing a mask. Someone complained about him disrupting the peace with his preaching. Apparently, he had been out here for a few days yelling the same message. I waited there a moment before leaving. What were they planning to do with a man who had nothing? I thought. What would they do when they saw his Abnormal was gone?

I headed to the bus stop that would take me straight home. Although I had some time before I would be breaking the law, I had overstayed the curfew my parents had set for me. I was lost in thought, as my pace slowed thinking about the incident with the homeless man. How could someone's Abnormal be cured? Lev was the only adult I had ever seen without the Abnormal, and now this guy. Who had cured him? Once I hit the street corner where the bus stop was, my face planted against someone, knocking me to the ground.

"I'm so sorry. Are you okay?" a male voice said as a hand reached out to me.

"No, I'm sorry." I avoided the help as I picked myself up. A young man stood before me, slightly older and much taller than I was.

"I was trying to get home before curfew. I should have been paying attention," I said, dusting off my pants as I looked up at him. I blinked a few times at the gray eyes staring back at me. Skin like cinnamon, and a smile revealing teeth like pearls. His black, wavy hair hung slightly above his eyes. He had no Abnormal spot in sight and hardly any evidence of a mask. If he walked into my school, every girl would begin drooling.

"Are you sure?"

"Am I sure what?"

"That you are okay. That was a big fall." He kneeled, picking up the books and papers that had fallen from my bag. "You dropped these." He stood with my bag and books in his hands. I looked down, realizing I had been staring a little too long. I took my books and bag from him, not even saying thank you. A smile twitched its way to my cheek as I tried my best not to look awkward.

"So, are you a student at Lukenic?" He tilted his head down to make eye contact.

"What?" I said, looking up at him then away again. "No, why would you think that?"

He picked up a pamphlet about Lukenic that was still on the ground.

"Oh, thanks." I took it from him. "My best friend just got accepted there," I said as I drew my gaze up to peek at him.

"Sorry if I scared you."

"I'm not scared," I answered quickly. A golden crest was on the left side of his jacket in the shape of a dragon. It was the same as the logo on the Lukenic pamphlet.

"So, are you a student at Lukenic?" I asked.

"I am."

"It's a pretty great school."

He gave a gentle smile at my lame compliment. "Well, I have to get going," I said, starting to walk.

"What's your name?" he asked, stopping me. He looked like he could be a model for the pamphlet, with his hands in his pockets and his rolled sleeves.

"It's Mae Meadows."

"Meadows? Hmm." He looked upward. "Are you related to Elliana and Jace Meadows?"

"Yes, they're my parents. You know them?" This was the second time today someone recognized my family name.

"They're Lukenic alumni."

"Oh, yeah. I forgot." I guessed it was normal for Lukenic students to know some of the alumni, but I didn't think my parents were big students there.

"So that means your grandfather is Niles Cefend?"

"Yeah," I said softly.

"I'm Fane Tache."

"Fane Tache?" I repeated.

"Yes, but Fane is fine." He continued to smile. "You know, with your family's track record, I would think you would continue with the tradition of being a Lukenic student. I bet you're just as smart as they are."

Smart was one thing I was never called. Mostly the opposite of smart.

"Well, I don't have the grades for Lukenic."

"Oh, well, grades aren't everything." He took a few steps toward me. "Because in the end, all that matters is how someone looks. Isn't that what we are taught, Miss Meadows?"

"You mean to hide the Abnormal?" I leaned in, zeroing in on his jaw. "Your mask is high-end. It looks very expensive."

His eye widened as he touched the side of his face.

"Oh," I said quickly. It was a bad habit of mine, trying to see the mask on people's faces.

He smirked, placing his hands back in his pocket.

"I do have to go," I said, stepping aside to pass him.

"It was nice to meet you, Mae. Maybe when you come to visit your friend at Lukenic, we'll meet again."

When I arrived home, the sound of multiple people speaking filtered though the door, but it got silent once I was inside. All eyes were on me as my aunt, cousins, and parents sat in the living room. "What's going on?" I asked as I removed my bag at the door.

"We're here visiting," Aunt Mary said. She sat next to my cousin, Marty. He was in his military uniform, standing like he was on duty. Marty was part of the Defense, which was a step higher than a Vigilant. He had been a normal kid the past year, but the person standing in the living room was an adult. He was four years older than me, but until he'd joined the Defense, he'd acted more like a thirteen-year-old.

My other cousin, Marcella, who was about a year old, sat in my aunt's lap.

Mom sat on the other side of Aunt Mary, rubbing her back, while Dad sat across from them. It was obvious that they were discussing Grandpa.

"How was school, Mae Flower?" Dad said, breaking the awkward silence.

"Um, I don't know," I responded. "Good, I guess. Rita got into Lukenic."

"That is excellent news," Dad said, looking at Mom.

"You almost missed curfew, Mae," Mom said, narrowing her eyes.

"I wanted to go for a walk before catching the bus. Sorry," I said, walking to the staircase that sat in the center of the house. I stepped up to the first step and leaned forward against the banister. "So," I started as I looked everywhere but at Mom. "Any news about Grandpa?" My aunt quickly looked at Mom, then at me.

"No, we haven't," Mom responded, glancing back at my aunt and sipping her tea.

"Mae, will you take Marcella upstairs? I know she'd been missing you," Mom said.

"Sure." I looked at Marty, who two years prior had been outside chasing me with a tissue filled with snot. I just hoped that a bit of kid was still in him. Maybe he would tell me what was going on. I walked over, hugged my aunt, and took Marcella into my arms. Aunt Mary smiled, then looked away.

I'd babysat for my aunt when Marcella was born. My uncle was hardly around because of his work, and my aunt needed extra help since Marty had joined the Defense. Marcella never made a fuss with me. She was chubby, cute, and had a head full of hair.

When I got to my room, I placed her down on her feet, and she walked directly to the bed, throwing her body against it. She turned her head to me with her bright brown eyes, a big smile, and dark curly hair like a halo. Marcella brought me joy, but it just wasn't enough to distract me from thinking about my grandfather.

I kept imagining him sitting in the living room, minding his business, as Vigilant rushed in, taking him away. Not even explaining why they were there.

I wondered how well the Chief Advisor knew Grandpa. I rarely heard anyone say anything positive about him. And he had described me as having a good imagination, too. I knew that must have thrown the teachers off.

My thoughts were interrupted by a knock at the door, and Marty peeked his head in.

"Hey, can I come in?" he said with a small smile.

"Of course. That uniform doesn't scare me."

Marty chuckled as he walked over to my bed and sat beside me. He was bigger than before, and much fitter. He used to be skinny, but the Defense had turned him into a man. I'd worried his new image would mean he wouldn't want to me around me anymore, but it seemed like I'd been wrong.

"So, what are they talking about? I know that I'm not allowed to hear it," I said.

"It's about Grandpa, obviously."

"I don't know why I had to leave the room."

"They just don't want to upset you."

"Why? Is there something I don't know?"

"It's complicated. You're just a kid, and they just don't want you to worry about anything."

"But I'm already worried."

"Exactly," he said, taking a deep breath and folding his arms.

"I'm almost fourteen," I said as I glared at him. "I can handle bad news."

"Ha!" Marty said, laughing at me. "Being fourteen doesn't mean anything."

"But you can tell me."

"Drop it, Mae."

"It's not fair," I said back. "Mom and Dad show up unexpectedly, then Grandpa is gone, and I'm supposed to accept that?"

"I think that was just a coincidence, Mae."

"Why did they take him?" I asked, pulling Marcella closer and holding her like a teddy bear. "You don't understand, Marty," I said, looking away. "It's really important that I see him."

"And why is that? Does it have something to do with you sneaking out of the house?"

I ignored his comment. "I just want to know that he's okay. I started blaming him for everything. For why I had no friends and why I was behind in my education. I completely stopped talking to him, too." I hated Eradeem. I felt like I had to choose between the man who raised me and loved me, and the city that only made me feel trapped. Marcella looked up at me like she knew how I was feeling.

"I'm sorry, Mae," Marty said, rubbing my back. "Maybe I can at least find out where he is for you. I doubt you could see him, but I know he means more to you than anyone in our family."

"Really? You can do that?"

"Yeah, I'm sure someone can give me a clue where he is, but I can't make any promises. I was already thinking of trying to find him myself. Perhaps go to see him if I can. Anyways, I came up to check on Marcella, since she isn't well these days."

"Why, what's wrong with her?"

"She's having Pains. Mom wanted me to make sure you knew that, just in case she has an episode."

"She has Pains already? Isn't she too young?"

"Yeah, it's pretty weird."

He took her from my arms, removed off her shirt, and laid her on her back.

"Keeping her cool helps reduce her Pains."

Pains were something that everyone went through as a child. It usually happened around three or four years of age. I had never heard of infants having them.

"Her mark would usually get warm right before the Pains start," Marty said.

He touched the grayish smudge on her chest right above her heart. I put my hand over my chest when I saw Marcella's mark. It looked as if someone had dipped their finger in gray powder and smeared it over her chest.

Seeing her small little mark reminded me of the story Lev had told me about the king, about the babies dying from the curse, and how the old man healed everyone. How the king healed Premleen.

"Marty, have you ever heard of anyone referring to the Abnormal as a curse before?"

Marty looked up, pausing. "Mom used to say that Grandma would call it that."

"Really? I'd never heard anyone say that before."

"Then why do you ask?"

"I was just wondering. I thought I heard it somewhere. So, I'm guessing you heard what happened over the weekend."

"Yeah, Grandpa got arrested, then you were missing, then somehow you snuck back home. What were you even doing outside so late?"

"Okay, so I didn't sneak home. I don't know how I got home. I went to Grandpa's base, because no one would tell me what happened to him."

"In the middle of the night?"

"I couldn't sleep and I wanted to find out for myself. I thought maybe something there would tell me what happened."

"Just letting you know, the discussion downstairs wasn't just about Grandpa; it was about you, too."

"I guess that makes sense. What are they saying?"

Marty gave a heavy sigh. "Look, Mae, just do your best to stay out of trouble."

"So, you aren't going to tell me?" I asked.

"Just take my advice, okay? Here." Marty took my hand, placing it on Marcella's chest. "Next time you have to watch Marcella, you've got to pay attention to how warm her chest gets." It felt warmer compared to the rest of her body.

When I was younger, I used to stare at my own mark all the time. I would try scrubbing it off with soap like it was dirt, thinking it would disappear. I just felt like it didn't belong there. My mark was a little smaller than Marcella's, which wasn't normal for someone my age. My dad's mark covered his whole chest, and Mom's seemed to go to her legs and arms. Mom never let me see her without her mask anymore, or without long pants and sleeves. Other than my own mark, Marcella's, and other kid's her age, I had only seen my parents'. Mom was lighter in complexion than Dad and me, so the mark was very noticeable on her.

"So is she going to be okay? Her spot's getting warm."

"She usually does well when she is sleeping."

"There was a song Grandma used to sing to me," I said as the words came to my mind. "She would hold me tight, rock me, and sing to me when I was having Pains." I closed my eyes, trying to remember the words, as the melody came to me first. I hummed it, and it started to come back to my memory.

I took Marcella in my arms like Grandma did with me and began to sing it to her.

glorious light
in a world darkened by fear
to shepherds revealed
on their faces yielding
did angels appear

orient sky
ablaze with stellary fire
sent to guide the flight
journey through the night
over mountains and mire
four centuries of silence
so long we've been waiting
for life to come and break us from this death

"Kind of a weird song to sing to a baby," Marty said.

"Yeah, it is." The words from that song were similar to the words found on the lanterns. It hadn't occurred to me until I heard myself singing them.

"What's a shepherd?" Marty asked.

"Someone who takes care of sheep," I said, rocking Marcella as I caressed her cheek with my thumb.

"What's a sheep?"

"It's an animal."

"How do you even know this?"

"I don't know."

Once Marty and Marcella left, I lay down on my side, singing that song. I closed my eyes, trying to remember what had happened over the weekend. I remembered Lev and the sheep. The hills, and the black sky, covered in stars. The smell of the air, and the sound of the night. If it was all a dream, I wanted to go back there again. It was nothing like anything I had ever experienced. I wished I could tell my parents about everything, but I knew they wouldn't listen, even if it was just a silly dream.

I was starting to feel alone, not having anyone to talk to. My grandfather and now my best friend were being taken from me.

I felt a hand on my head, making me jump from my daydream. Mom was sitting on my bed.

"I'm sorry," Mom said as she pulled away. "I didn't mean to startle you. I heard you singing that old song. I can't believe you even remember it."

"Marty said Marcella started having Pains; I thought singing to her could help. Why does she have to go through that? Isn't she too young?"

"I don't know, to be honest. No one knows why we have Pains in the first place."

A part of Mom's shoulder was bare, revealing her Abnormal. It looked different. More textured and darker than before.

"Do you think it's a curse?"

"Do I think what's a curse?" Mom asked.

"Pains, and Abnormal?" I clarified. She noticed me staring at her shoulder, and she immediately covered it up.

"What makes you say that?"

"Marty said Grandma called it a curse."

"There is no such thing as a curse. Mom was from the old times; they believed a lot of stuff."

"Did they believe in stars?" I asked. She paused for a moment, giving me a questioning look.

"Grandpa was still talking about stars with you, huh?"

"No, I'm just asking."

"Mae, I thought we talked about this. I thought you were finally over that star crap. You're too old even to be thinking about that. You're not a baby anymore."

"If I'm not a baby anymore, why can't you tell me why Grandpa was taken away?"

Her expression was blank as she turned to the window.

"We can talk about this at a different time," Mom said, leaving the room.

Nine

After Rita got accepted into Lukenic, she never returned to school. It was close to the end of the school year, so it kind of made sense, though it frustrated me. I wanted to pick her brain about what she remembered, but I couldn't seem to get in touch with her. Rumors were spreading about what had happened that weekend. One day, some boy came up to me asking if I ran away from home and if Grandpa killed someone. Rita's absence only made the rumors worse.

About two weeks after the incident, the teachers turned on the TVs in every classroom to show us the inauguration of the new leader, President Odoman. As usual, no one knew who the Counsel of Reason would select as the president after a previous leader died. We watched the ceremony and listened to the new leader's speech. I was excited to see the Chief Advisor appear to introduce and congratulate Odoman, even though his expression was stone-cold like last time I'd seen him.

I spent most of the class, however, thinking about Lev and the story he'd told me. My parents forbade me from going back to Grandpa's base, but when they weren't paying attention, I had. I wanted to see if the lanterns Rita and I found were real. Everything at the base was as before. Grandpa's lanterns were just as we had left them, and the one from the sky was still in the middle of the field. I was too afraid to go off into the woods alone, not even to look for my shoes and the doll I had lost. I wondered if Grandpa had experienced similarly weird things before he was taken.

I hardly noticed my teacher standing there, looking down her nose at me. She snatched the paper off my desk to see what I was doing. Her disappointment worsened when she saw it was mostly doodles of stars and sheep. "Looks like you aren't focused at all, Miss Meadows. You didn't hear me calling your name this whole time?"

"Sorry. I thought this wasn't an actual assignment," I said, smiling, trying to appear innocent.

She unconsciously rubbed at the slightly peeled mask underneath her jaw. "Whether this is for a grade or not, you need to pay attention. You've been called to the office. Take all your things and follow Mr. Owns." She pointed at the strange man who stood by the door. I'd never seen him before; he definitely wasn't a member of staff. He was wearing a black suit and black tie, with tiny, tinted glasses. He was looking right at me, sternly, with his hands behind his back.

I stood, gathered my things, and followed my instructor, who handed my paper full of doodles to him, and then whispered something. The other students only stared as I left the room with the man. I wasn't sure if I was in trouble or if something had happened to my family. The hallway felt more silent than normal. I was afraid to ask where I was going or why I was being pulled out of class. We reached the administrative office and headed to the principal's room. When I entered, the principal was nowhere in sight. A woman was sitting in his seat, with another man dressed like Mr. Owns in a chair against the wall across from her.

"Have a seat," she said, pointing at the chair in front of her desk.

"Okay." I looked back at Mr. Owns, who handed the paper with my sketches to the woman at the desk. The only light came from the window behind the woman, making it difficult to see her. Her rectangular glasses had a white glare that blocked her eyes; but still, I felt her gaze on me the whole time.

"Miss Mae Meadows," the woman began. "I'm Ms. Vivly."

"Did I do something wrong?" I asked.

"Well, that depends on if you are a truth-teller. We just want to ask you some questions. Is that okay?" But before I could respond, she continued.

"We already spoke with Rita Manna, and she gave us some very interesting information about Niles Cefend, your grandfather."

I felt a cold sweat under my arms and a pounding in my chest. Grandpa? What was going on? What did Rita do?

"W-what did she say?"

"We want you to tell us," Ms. Vivly said.

"I—I don't know. Is it about his star research?" I asked.

"Yes, stars. We can start there. So, what do you know about stars?"

"I know they aren't real."

"Really? I was told there were complaints from your teachers in the previous years about you and stars."

"Yes, I do—I mean, I did used to be interested in that kind of stuff," I answered. "But it doesn't mean that I thought it was a real thing." I felt my books and notebook about to fall from my lap. I grabbed them and clenched them to my chest, praying that another stupid drawing wouldn't show.

"I was childish back then, and I fantasized a lot, but I've grown out of that. It was just a phase."

"But Niles, your grandfather, was the one who influenced you in that kind of behavior, am I right?"

"I don't know what you mean?"

"Your grandfather has a history of wasting time and money on research that went nowhere. He had to step down from the Union of Cognition. And I'm sure that, even after explaining to him the dangers of spreading misinformation, he still chose to keep talking about his fantasies. Spreading lies to children, in my opinion, is more dangerous than his research on stars."

I glanced back to the man, who was now writing, likely recording the conversation.

"So, Mae, did your grandfather ever talk to you about stars?"

"Why is my grandpa in jail?" I asked, trying to change the subject.

Ms. Vivly took a deep breath and slouched in her chair.

"We believe your grandfather planned some kind of rebellion against Eradeem, and maybe you were involved."

"Rebellion? That's not true!" I protested.

"Then where were you that Friday evening when your grandfather was arrested?"

"I was with Rita."

"Where?"

"Out for a walk."

"So, it was the middle of the night, you and Rita were going for a walk?"

"Yes, then I got lost."

"You know you're supposed to be inside by eight p.m.?"

"I don't know?" I responded.

"Rita mentioned that you met someone out in the woods," Ms. Vivly continued.

"No, I mean, I had a dream that I met someone."

"Dream?"

"Yes, I dreamed that I was outside Eradeem talking to a man who told me I was hundreds of miles from home. Sheep surrounded me, and I could see Eradeem, far away." I stopped.

Ms. Vivly paused for a moment, staring at me. She leaned forward, causing the glare from her glasses to disappear. "Sheep?" she asked, tilting her head. "And what is a sheep?"

"Um… I don't know."

"Miss Mae Meadows, it seems like your rebellion against the rules set to keep you safe isn't just going to cause the destruction of your family, but may also have corrupt your mind. This was clearly a hallucination of some kind."

"Why would I be hallucinating, and what does my family have to do with this?" I asked.

"The curfew is to protect you from the toxins across our border." She straightened up in her chair. "It has a drastic effect on the young and old. At night, toxins can seep into the city. Although their effects aren't as strong as in the past, we still like to stay cautious. The outside world is dangerous. You and your family are some of the few people who live that close to the border.

"We do a good job of protecting our city from it, so there is no need to make the public aware of the toxic results— but for a very small percentage of people, they cause hallucinations. If you follow the law, these toxins are nothing to worry about. However, if you don't, well… We believe they're one of the reasons why your grandfather is so sick. At some point, he must have been exposed to chemicals, perhaps even on multiple occasions. Where your home is now is a safe distance from the border, but we believe he has gone out farther than he should. We suspect, because of something he saw in a hallucination, your grandfather planned to release those toxins into the city. He believes doing so will allow all in Eradeem to see stars as he feels he has."

"I didn't realize that," I said.

"It's not something you have to worry yourself about if you are following the laws set in place to keep you protected."

"So, this is why you wanted to know what happened over the weekend?"

"Of course. And, one more thing. About your parents," Ms. Vivly said.

"My parents? What about them?"

"Like your grandfather, we suspect that one of them is dabbling in work they were not assigned."

"My parents are always away from home. And neither one of them ever talked about stars or believed they're real."

"Uh-huh, well, that is good to hear."

"If you have a problem with them, you can just ask them yourself." It was weird that she was asking me these questions as if I were the parent, and my parents were my children.

"It's my job to keep Eradeem youth safe, whether someone has good intentions or not; most people don't understand the impact that disobedience could have on our society."

The final bell rang to release us from school as Ms. Vivly adjusted her glasses, looking at the clock. "If you have nothing else to share with me, you are free to leave."

I got up from my seat and left without a second thought. So, I had finally gotten some answers about why Grandpa was arrested, yet I wasn't sure how to take them. Grandpa had never mentioned actually seeing stars to me. Was it something he'd only talked about among colleagues? Did they report him for his claims? Could it be true that he was planning to release toxins into the city? Could I have been affected by the toxins, too?

I knew, now, that I had to talk to Rita. After school, I ran to her house. I wanted to know if she'd had any strange dreams or hallucinations since I last saw her. And I had to know what she'd told Ms. Vivly.

It didn't take me long to get there. After catching my breath outside of her fence, I pushed through the white picket gate leading to her double door. I knocked, trying my best not to seem frantic. But my palms were sweaty, and I was worried they wouldn't hear me. So, I knocked again, a bit louder. The door opened while I was on my second knock, and Rita's mother appeared.

"Sorry," I said quickly. Rita's mom had one hand on her hip, the other holding the doorknob. I peeked around to see if Rita was nearby.

"Is there a problem, Mae?" She towered over me.

"Um, no. Not exactly," I said, looking toward the ground. "I was just wondering about Rita. I wondered if she was okay since she hasn't been at school for a couple days. Can I see her?"

"Well, right now she isn't seeing anyone."

"Oh."

"She is preparing for Lukenic, and she can't be distracted."

"Is she going to come back to our school?"

"No, I don't think so," she said, almost cutting me off. "Is there anything else?"

"Well, is it possible that I can talk to her just for a moment? It's very important."

"If you have anything you want to talk to Rita about, you can tell me, and I will give her your message." Rita's mother had always been strict with her, but at that moment, she was beyond strict. She had never treated me like this. I was shocked.

"I guess it can wait for another time. But if you could tell…"

"Actually, Mae," Rita's mom interrupted. "I don't think there will be another time. I learned about your grandfather's arrest and the lies he has put into my daughter's head, almost destroying her future. And I don't know what kind of teaching your family is giving you, but I can no longer have you around Rita."

"What lies?"

"Rita has been working too hard not to get into Lukenic." And without warning, Rita's mom closed the door in my face. I blinked, staring at it. What just happened? What did Rita tell them? I took a step back as my thoughts raced, wondering how bad their family thought I was. What was this lie Rita believed that was scaring her parents? Did I just lose my one and only friend? I took in a deep breath, nodding to myself as I turned away.

"It's okay," I said, walking to the gate. I looked back at the top left window of the house, where Rita's room was. Someone stood there. I was sure it was Rita looking down at me.

Ten

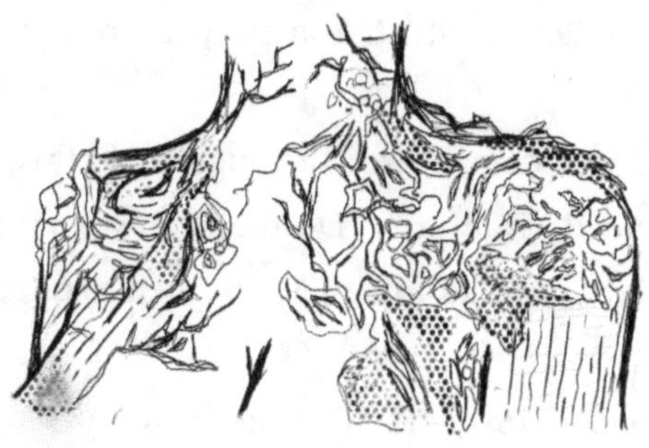

When I arrived home, my parents were fighting upstairs. I went straight into my room, collapsing on my bed. Mom was doing most of the yelling, and Dad was defending himself. I didn't want to listen, but I could hear everything. They were arguing about Mom's project. Dad believed she was going too far and that she was hurting herself. I thought about what Ms. Vivly said: that one of my parents was involved in an assignment they were not supposed to be doing. Was it Mom?

"I told you this would happen!" I heard Mom stepping out into the hallway. It was clear they didn't know I was home.

"You are going to ruin this family. Then where will we be, Jace? Because you won't listen!"

"Look at you. Are you seeing this?" Dad shouted back. "You're the one who is changing, and you think you can hide it with the stupid mask. There is no makeup or anything that is going to cover this up, and you're concerned about me?"

"I can handle this. I don't need your help," Mom yelled back. "Stick to the assignment they gave you."

"You're my wife! What kind of man would I be if I watched you go through this alone? There must be a way to fix this."

"Don't do that," Mom interrupted. "They entrusted me with this research because I can handle it. You aren't even supposed to know about it."

"I never said you weren't strong enough to do this, but you need help. Do they know?" Dad said. "Do they know what this project is doing to you?" I heard Dad follow Mom, then pause at my slightly opened door.

"You're acting like my dad. Thinking I'm too weak. Thinking I'm not smart enough for this project. I know what I am doing."

"Your dad? Is that what this is all about? Are you trying to prove something?"

My dad looked into my room and saw me inside. He closed my bedroom door, but I got up and cracked it open, peeking through. Dad pulled Mom to the end of the hallway, facing her with his back to me.

"What are you talking about?" Mom yelled.

"Lower your voice. We don't need to bring Mae into this."

"Does it matter at this point? She'll find out sooner or later. She should have been in boarding school, and none of this would have happened. I let Dad convince me that he could raise her, even knowing he believes the lies mom used to feed me."

"So, is that why you sent him away?" Dad said, trying to lower his voice. "Or was it because he kept warning you about what the Abnormal was doing to you? You reported him out of pride. Because no matter how much you try to convince yourself he lost his mind, you know he's right about the Abnormal."

"How dare you! I did it for his own good. He is sick; he needs help."

"He was fine here at home with Mae, Elliana."

"You call that fine, with all the issues she was having in school? That's okay with you?"

"She's changed drastically. Her education isn't an issue anymore."

"You think so? I know better than anyone how my mother's teachings can get in your head and affect you for years. They are the reason I was so confused for such a long time growing up. I'm not going to continue letting him do that to Mae. He needed to go."

"You didn't," I said. I found myself outside my bedroom, standing in the middle of the hallway, watching my parents. They both looked back at me like they had lost their words.

"They took him because of you. You reported your own father?" I said with my eyes fixated on her, but she didn't respond.

"Mae, you weren't supposed to find out like this," Dad said, stepping toward me.

"Are you going to report us, too?" I said to Mom. Dad paused, standing between us. Mom looked over at me, at Dad, then left us in the hall as she went into her office.

"Don't say that, Mae," Dad said. But I didn't respond; I only stared at him and then turned back into my room, slamming the door behind me.

"How could she?" I said, throwing myself onto my bed. I tried to breathe, but I felt myself choking from anger as I screamed into my pillow. I wasn't supposed to hear that. Since Grandpa's arrest, life was miserable. Everything seemed to be getting worse, and it was because of her. I wished I had stayed home instead of going to the woods that night.

I started to wonder if I wasn't okay. If Grandpa and I were affected by the chemicals on the other side of the border. Could she quickly get rid of me like she did Grandpa if I was hallucinating from getting too close to the border? Meeting with Ms. Vivly only made my desire to see Rita more necessary. I needed someone to remind me of what had happened that night. What was real, and what wasn't? I had proof of the floating lantern from the sky, but I still needed more evidence I wasn't losing my mind. Was Rita suffering from hallucinations, too? Maybe that was what her mother had meant about lies Rita was telling her.

I looked over the side of my bed and saw Rita's camera was slightly under it. I had forgotten to return it to her, and I hadn't looked at it since the night I got lost. I tried to turn it on, hoping there'd be something on the camera to help me clear my mind, but it immediately died. All of our batteries were in Mom's office, and the last thing I wanted was to talk to her after finding out what she did to Grandpa. I peeked out of the room to check whether she'd retreated to her bedroom. Her office seemed to be clear, so I snuck in and quickly searched for batteries, finding exactly what I needed.

As I walked back to my room, I could hear Mom in the bedroom. She was crying. I could tell she was trying to be quiet, but there was pain in her voice. I thought about what she had said. She felt like she had been suffering her whole life because of Grandma, and she didn't want me to go through the same experience. She probably got bullied at school, too, when she talked about the things Grandma told her. I didn't want to care about her right then, but I could understand why she felt the way she did. She was just trying to protect me. I paused at her door, wondering if I should go in. I knocked, but she didn't respond. Steeling myself, I went in.

The room was dark and empty; the only light came from the bathroom to the left. Mom was there with the door slightly open. She moaned as I caught her reflection in the mirror. I stepped into the room, then paused. She had taken off her shirt and removed the mask from her arms. But something else was in the bathroom with her. I moved closer to get a better look. It was like a large leather bag, but it moved like it was alive. Mom appeared again in the mirror, this time having taken the mask off her face. She had soft gray patches on her cheeks and forehead.

As she peeled the artificial skin from below her chin to her collarbone, I saw that she was dark and hardened. She moved near the door, and I jerked backward. Dark, hard blotches covered her back. Her body looked scaly, reptilian.

I pulled back against the doorframe slowly as my heart thumped against my chest at the sight of her. I had never seen anything like it in my life. Then I remembered the documents in Mom's office. The one she took from me right before she pulled me out of the room. The document had a subtitle reading "Abnormal 3", with pictures of people who did not look fully human. Were those pictures of her?

I couldn't imagine talking to her now; I was too shaken. I did my best to leave without being noticed and returned to my room. I closed the door, leaning against it as I slid to the ground. I squeezed my eyes shut, trying to push the image of my mom out of my head. What was going on? Was this normal? Was this what Mom and Dad were fighting about? What was happening to her?

I hardly ever saw my parents without their masks, especially my mom. Was this Abnormal 3? I'd never heard anything about it in school. Seeing her in the bathroom, it was clear that the Abnormal was changing her, coming up to her face, down her back, and all over her body. Dad seemed like he was trying to do something about Mom's Abnormal, but Mom refused any help from him. I wondered if anyone she worked with knew what was happening to her. I let my head fall back against the door, staring at the glowing lights Grandpa and I had painted on the ceiling when I was eight, feeling the tears fall from the corners of my eyes. I really wished that I was somewhere else.

I distracted myself by putting the batteries in the camera. It turned on, and I navigated through it mindlessly until I saw a lantern. I took a deep breath, closing my eyes. "This is real." I found a picture of a trail of lights in the sky, just like I had seen that night. I went to the next picture of the lantern that was above me, coming down while the fire burned inside. "That happened," I said, studying the photo.

I didn't remember taking any more photos that night; the lanterns should have been the last ones. I started going back through the pictures I passed through. A lot of them were just black. I kept going until I got to the last photo, which was mostly bright and blurry. I could tell someone was in it because I could see legs. I zoomed in more, studying it, trying to see who it was. Their hands were covering their face from the camera, trying to block the light. I gasped. It was a picture of Lev.

Eleven

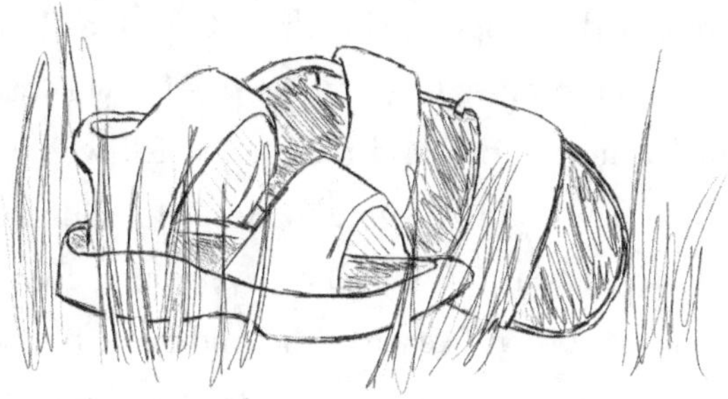

As I stared at Lev's picture, all I could hear was the pounding of my own heart. I zoomed in on the smallest part that revealed a face, trying to tell myself it was someone else. I hadn't intended to take his picture, but I thought I knew when it happened. He came out of nowhere from the woods, scaring me half to death. I remembered him blocking the light from the camera and helping me off the ground. Nothing that happened that night made sense, but it was clear, now, that it wasn't a dream.

I was a bit fearful of going back to find the place I fell, but I needed a little bit more proof that everything that happened was real. Leaving at that moment was the best thing. I figured my parents wanted their space and, hopefully, wouldn't come checking on me for a while.

I took a jacket and Rita's camera in case I needed to take pictures again.

I pushed Mom out of my mind, trying to focus. I grabbed a flashlight and headed into the woods on the path to Grandpa's base.

I wasn't sure what my plan was, but something in me needed to go back to the place where I'd met Lev, back to where the stars were. I needed to know who Lev was. I only hoped I would see him again. As I got deeper into the woods, the red lights of Eradeem began to fade.

I finally reached the open field where Grandpa's base was, but my body didn't want to move forward. No one knew I was out there. Waiting until the morning to find the place I fell would have been wiser, but I knew I wouldn't be able to sleep if I didn't continue. I was desperate for answers, so I pushed everything from my mind and moved forward. When I reached the middle of the field, I tried to remember exactly what part of the woods I had entered. Retracing my steps, I looked to the sky over the trees, trying to reimagine the lanterns and where they were coming from. I picked a spot that felt right and walked, keeping my eyes on the sky.

When I looked back at the city from afar, Eradeem was like a burning furnace. I slowed down around the spot I thought the glowing bugs were. I walked in that direction, but there wasn't a bug in sight. I was careful with my steps, keeping my flashlight pointed downward so I wouldn't fall like last time. I remembered the hill being wide, but I had no clue if I was in the right place. I took a deep breath and continued walking. When I thought I had gone too far,

I turned around, changing my direction. Still, there was no hill. How could I miss something as steep as the slope I plummeted from? It could easily be mistaken as a small cliff. I continued moving forward, watching my steps. Looking around, I tried to remember if anything looked familiar, anything that would give me a clue.

But the truth was I never did find my way out of the woods that night. Running around that evening alone, it felt like hours had passed before Lev found me. Seeing stars, meeting Lev, and seeing the animals were all so strange, but even weirder was how I could be miles away from Eradeem after a fall. How could I have teleported to the outside, I thought.

"No, that's crazy," I said, freezing in my tracks as I slapped my cheeks.

"There's no such thing as teleportation." There has to be an explanation." The thought made me feel like perhaps the toxins Miss Vivly mentioned were real. Maybe I was being affected by it now? I took a hard gulp at the thought. Even so, I had proof that someone was in the woods with me from Rita's camera. And I was determined to figure this out. I continued walking; then, suddenly, I lost my balance. Something in that step rolled under my foot, making me hit the ground, but I didn't tumble down a hill this time.

"My shoes!" I shouted, looking over to where I tripped. Somehow, I made it to the place where I lost my sandals. I don't remember when they slipped off. Suppose it was before I tumbled down the hill. I took hold of them as I stood up quickly.

"This is the place," I said, pointing the flashlight around me. But the ground was flat.

"What is going on? Something should have changed by now," I said to myself. I heard someone or something else in the woods with me. I pointed my flashlight toward the sound. As I got closer to it, I saw a light beaming through the treetops from afar.

The ground started to feel softer as I walked closer. I reached down, feeling sand mixed with grass.

I made it to a steep hill where the wood finally ended and saw, at the bottom, a large concrete wall through which light was seeping. I found the tree closest to the hill and hid behind it. There were a few men on top of the wall with guns, walking around the barbed wire.

This was the border.

I ran to the next tree ahead to get a closer look at the wall. The men guarding it were in military uniforms, the same that Marty wore. I moved to the next tree, trying my best to stay out of sight. There weren't many soldiers, just two men standing every five hundred yards or so, in front of the doors in the wall. I peeked out and saw that the wall went on forever. We were told that everything beyond the border was desert. I wondered how I could possibly get outside of Eradeem without passing through this wall first.

"Hey!" a voice shouted from behind me, and I fell forward. "What are you doing?"

I turned over to a man standing above me with a gun pointed at me, a light shining from it. I threw my hands over my face. "Please don't shoot me!" I yelled. As if, somehow, I could block any potential bullets coming my way. "I'm sorry, I'm sorry," I repeated.

"What the heck are you doing this far in the woods, huh?" the man yelled, lowering his gun. "Do you know what time it is? I know you aren't old enough to be out this late. You aren't supposed to be out here."

"I know, just please don't hurt me; I can go home immediately, just don't shoot."

"Nobody's gonna kill you; get up." He took me by the arm, pulling me to my feet. "Hey, I found some kid out here," he shouted. He took me by my arm and walked me out of the woods toward the wall.

"Mae?" a voice called. I looked over to see Marty standing to the side.

"You know this girl, Marty?" the man said, yanking me by my arm.

"Yes, she's my cousin."

"Why is she out here? Civilians aren't supposed to be out here."

"Well ..." Marty hesitated. "She's out here because I asked her to come."

"What! For what?" the soldier asked, narrowing his eyes at Marty.

"She doesn't live far from here, so I told her to bring me some lunch. Her parents are scientists— you know the types who live in these parts."

"Really," the man said.

"Yes," Marty replied.

"So, where's your lunch?"

"She already gave it to me." Marty walked toward me, taking my arm from the soldier's grip. "I'll make sure she goes home for good this time. I shouldn't have had her come out here—I won't ask again."

Marty walked away from the scene, pulling me along. I could hardly keep up with him as he quickly entered the woods.

"What the heck are you doing out here, Mae?" He stopped and turned to me once we were out of sight. "You're going to get us in trouble." He looked behind me to ensure no one was around.

"I was just going for a walk."

"A walk? You know you are not supposed to be out in the woods. What's going on, Mae?"

What was I supposed to tell him? I glanced up at our starless sky, wishing I could tell Marty everything.

"What are you looking at?" Marty said, following my gaze.

"Nothing," I answered.

"So, you aren't going to tell me anything, huh?"

He continued walking me back to Grandpa's base, trying to get answers from me, but I wouldn't speak about why I was out there.

Once we reached the field where Grandpa's base was, Marty stopped. He couldn't go too far off since he was working.

"Before you go, I have something to tell you. I found out where Grandpa is."

"You did?" I said, quickly turning to him.

"I'm actually supposed to be working there tomorrow."

"Are you serious?" I took Marty's arm, hugging it tightly.

"I thought you would want to hear that."

"Of course I want to hear. So, how is he? Is he okay?" I questioned, shifting my weight from side to side.

"As far as I know, he's fine."

"So, when are we going to see him?"

"It's just going to be me, Mae," Marty said, pulling away from me.

"There's no way for me to see him?"

"I'm not a hundred percent sure if I can see him myself, but I can at least report back to the family on how he's doing. Mom hasn't been well since finding out about his arrest."

"I finally found out why Grandpa was taken," I said, looking away from Marty.

"Did your parents tell you?"

"I overheard them talking about it. It was Mom. She had him arrested because she thinks he's sick. A woman from school said that he had some plans against Eradeem."

Marty took a deep breath but didn't respond.

"I don't know why you couldn't tell me that," I said, looking back at him.

"Who knows how you would have taken that news. You might investigate what he was trying to do. But looks like you're doing that anyway," Marty said.

"Can you make a way for me to see him, please?"

"You won't tell me why you came out here. Why should I do this for you?"

"You're going to think I'm crazy."

"What is it?"

"Well…" I tried to sort out what I should share. "I wanted to retrace my steps from when I got lost last time because…" I paused, letting my eyes wander anywhere but to him.

"I saw stars in the sky the night Grandpa was arrested."

"You saw stars?" Marty replied.

"I thought I could find the place where I'd been and maybe see them again. Just don't tell anyone, okay?"

"You do sound crazy," Marty said, letting out a big sigh.

"I know, and I know about the chemicals over the border, too. I just found out today."

"Then why would you come this far out? I've been trained and tested to handle anything from over the border."

"Do you think I have been affected?" I asked Marty.

"Seems like it, since you claim to see something that doesn't exist. As far as Grandpa, I can't make any promises, but I will see what I can do."

"Thanks," I said, taking him in for a last hug.

"Just be patient."

"Okay, I'll try." I wondered if Grandpa had seen Lev, too. Did whatever he was supposedly planning have to do with him? As I turned to leave, I was left with a disturbing feeling in my gut.

"Marty!" I yelled as he walked away. "Before I go, can you answer a question for me?"

"What is it?"

"That wall, has it always been there?" I asked.

"Of course, it's our border; it's always been here."

"Oh, so have you been to the other side?"

"Not really, only through the doors for maintenance purposes. It is a great structure. It borders the city from one end to the other. Why do you want to know?" he replied.

"No reason, just curious."

Twelve

When school finally ended that year, I spent my time mostly in my room. I never tried to get ahold of Rita again. It only seemed fair for her to reach out to me since I wasn't allowed over to her place. Eventually, she came by, but it was only to pick up her camera. I wanted to talk with her about the picture taken of Lev, but she had no time, since her mom was in the car waiting for her. Luckily, I'd printed out the pictures of Lev and the lanterns.

My parents had been officially working from home since Grandpa was taken. If they spoke to each other at all, they were fighting. I tried to avoid being around them, but I couldn't help but listen in sometimes after learning about Mom's condition. Most of their fighting was about work or Grandpa; the conflict over Mom's Abnormal seemed to be something they were avoiding. Still, I could tell Mom's condition was getting worse. Sometimes she looked as though her clothes were so uncomfortable they were causing her pain. Most days, she wouldn't come out of her room. Dad stayed downstairs, usually working, and slept in Grandpa's room.

I spent a lot of time drawing in my room during the break. But I also returned to Grandpa's base, studying the old children's book he'd left on his desk before he was taken. I read it repeatedly, trying to find clues. Even though it was in a different language, I swore that just looking at the pictures seemed to tell the story Lev told me. I tried my best to understand Grandpa's lousy handwriting in the notes, but had no luck. Sometimes I would just lie in bed, close my eyes, pull up an image of that night, and then try to re-create what I saw by drawing it.

I tried to remember the smells in the air and the soft wind that gently blew in my hair. The warmth of the fire and Lev's voice, which seemed to enchant the flames. I used the photograph I had of Lev, doing my best to draw his face. Re-creating the moment of him sitting across from me with the fire between us. I had proof that I did see Lev; I just wasn't sure about the rest of that night.

A month had passed since I had been caught near the border. I was relieved that I never heard anything about Marty getting in trouble over it. I was looking through the children's book one day when I was pulled away by the sound of a car driving up to our house. We usually didn't get many visitors besides my aunt, uncle, and Marty, so I thought it might be Marty bringing some news about Grandpa.

I went over to my window hoping to see him, but my heart stopped when I realized it was Ms. Vivly and Mr. Owns. "What the heck are they doing here?" I asked myself.

There was a knock on the door downstairs. What reason did they have to come to my house? I couldn't help but think it had something to do with me. My mind raced to remember if I'd said anything that would bring them to my home. I could hear Dad stepping out to greet them. I went over, peeking out the door. Dad shook their hands with what looked like a nervous smile, but Ms. Vivly and Mr. Owens looked just as serious as they had the first time. Mom was standing near the door, holding it open for them, as Dad walked in. I could smell that Mom had cooked something sweet.

I had never told my parents about Ms. Vivly coming to my school and questioning me about them and Grandpa. Mom greeted them, leading them to the living room. I walked from my room, moving closer to the staircase, trying to hear what was happening. Mom went into the kitchen, then brought back tea and cookies for them. I tried my best to be quiet so that I could hear.

"I think this will be the best for your family, Ms. Meadows," Ms. Vivly said.

"Well, we understand your concerns, what with my father's arrest and his history," Mom responded.

"Yes, it is my job to ensure that our future will be in the hands of responsible and intelligent young people," Ms. Vivly replied. "With the new school year starting soon, this will be the best opportunity for us to improve Mae's education. So, I'm happy to hear you are on board with the program."

"Of course," Mom replied. Dad stayed silent the whole time.

Were they sending me to a different school, or maybe something worse? I knew my parents loved me despite their conflict with each other. I couldn't imagine that they would want to harm me.

"Mae!" Mom called. I jumped, almost not breathing. I didn't respond, and I didn't want to. "Can you come down here?" she called as she appeared at the staircase. "Oh, there you are."

I froze. Mom's eyes met mine, but her expression was the same as usual: blank and unreadable.

"Come down, Mae; we have guests here. They have some things they want to talk to us about," Mom said.

"Am I in trouble?" I spoke faintly, just loud enough for Mom to hear. I took hold of the rail, my body stiffening.

"Just come down, Mae," Mom said, breaking eye contact with me. I took in what felt like my last breath as I let go of the rail to come downstairs. Dad sat on the sofa against the staircase; I sat next to him as Mom followed, sitting on the other side of me. Ms. Vivly and Mr. Owns sat in a chair across from us. Dad placed his arm around me, pulling me close. I looked at him as he rubbed my shoulder. He glanced back at me and then looked straight forward.

"It's good to see you again, Mae," Ms. Vivly started. "You remember me from school, I hope."

"Yes," I replied.

"Don't worry, your parents are aware of our meeting, but that isn't why I am here." Ms. Vivly kept her eyes on me, taking a sip of her tea. She had added no sugar or cream, and didn't even touch the cookies.

"Your parents and I know you have been out past curfew on more than one occasion. I was notified that you were discovered near Eradeem's border not too long ago."

My mouth dried as I tried to swallow nothing. I had hoped Marty would have kept that a secret, but he probably had to explain to his boss why I was found that far out in the woods.

Dad looked over at me. "Is that true, Mae?"

I confessed, lowering my head. They asked me why, but I couldn't find anything to tell them. Ms. Vivly instantly accused Grandpa of inspiring my bad behavior. She knew I was hiding something. She brought up how I was behind in school and how my teachers had complained about me disrupting the classroom.

"As Eradeem's Superintendent of Education, I make sure that every child is educated properly so that they can develop a healthy mind. This is because of Niles, I am sure. It wasn't wise to have him in charge of raising your child, given his history with the Union of Cognition."

"You know my father is a brilliant man," Mom started. "I still believe his positive history outweighs the negative. But I admit I didn't think his ideas would affect Mae so much. I've spoken to him serval times about side projects, and sharing them with Mae, but…" My mother paused, looking over at me, then back to Ms. Vivly. "I guess I underestimated how bad things were."

Ms. Vivly finished her tea, laying her cup down. She pulled out a black folder from her bag and handed it over to Dad. "This is where we are planning to send your daughter. Instead of going to Charper High School this year, she will be going to a special program we have for students like her in Lukenic."

"Lukenic?" I said, almost shouting. I was totally confused. "But I thought that Lukenic was for students with high grades."

"It is," Ms. Vivly responded. "But you will not be with those students. This program was created to get students like you back on track. Because of your family being a part of the Counsel of Reason and having a history at the school, we thought it would be a good fit. You will be living on campus, and believe me, no one will think you have earned your way to Lukenic. You will be placed on a different part of campus, away from the other students. There has been much damage done to you, and I am here to make sure it can be reversed."

"How are they going to do that exactly?" Dad responded.

"Just some reeducation. We don't want any child left behind," Ms. Vivly said. "It's going to be fine. It's for the best. The Lukenic school year starts earlier than other institutions," Ms. Vivly continued. "So, your summer break is going to be shorter than you are used to. This isn't a punishment, I assure you, even if it may seem like it is."

"I guess I don't get a say in this," I replied. My hands were folded tightly in my lap as I stared down at them. Who I was as a person, my interests, and what I believed were only causing problems in my life. What was so wrong with me that my family had to send me away?

"I'm sorry, Mae, but you don't have a choice. Tomorrow will be your first day," Ms. Vivly replied.

"What?" I said, shooting my eyes at Ms. Vivly. "Why now? Did you guys already know about this?" I shouted, looking over at Dad. He moved his arm away from me, looking over with a tightened smile and brow. "Sorry, Mae." That was all he could say.

"This isn't fair. Just because I made a couple of mistakes, you're sending me away." I turned to Mom, but she didn't look at me, only toward the ground.

"You shouldn't blame your parents, Mae," Ms. Vivly stated. "They're doing their best and want the best for you."

All I wanted to do was run from that house, to get as far away as possible. It was like no one was looking out for me, even if they believed they were.

"Why didn't anyone tell me?" I cried. Dad pulled me into his arms, only causing me to cry harder.

"Mae Flower," Dad said, rubbing my head.

"I asked your parents not to share this information with you," Ms. Vivly said. "I didn't want to have a young girl trying to run away from home." As Ms. Vivly continued to talk, her voice became muffled. I was filled with rage. My parents had betrayed me, and I felt like I had no one now.

Once Ms. Vivly and Mr. Owns left, my parents tried to talk to me, but I bolted to my room, slamming the door. I fell to my bed, wishing I could run away, but where would I go? They had placed Vigilant around our property so that I couldn't leave.

I screamed into my pillow, wailing till it hurt. I heard Dad yelling, blaming Mom for sending me away; and heard Mom blaming Grandpa for filling my head with lies. I'd lost my best friend, and Grandpa, and I guessed I would lose myself next. I drained myself from crying until I fell asleep. It was the only thing I could do to prepare for my new boarding school prison.

Thirteen

I slept through the night, waking to the sound of my mom searching my closet and dresser. I rose, sitting up straight, wiping my swollen eyes, confused about why she was in my room. Memories of yesterday flooded back. Mom looked over at me, then turned to the window next to my bed, staring off.

"I know you probably hate me." She sat on my bed, holding one of my shirts. She was right; I did hate her. I wanted nothing more than to tell her. I wanted to tell her how I knew that the Abnormal was changing her—not just on the outside, but on the inside, too. I wanted to tell her that she was a monster for reporting Grandpa. She didn't even cry when he was taken. But I couldn't say those things to her.

I remembered her being compassionate when I was younger. What had happened? As I got older, I learned that Eradeem always got the last word.

"I'm sorry that things are suddenly changing." She tried to look me in the eye, but I refused her. "I wish we could be more honest with you." Mom reached to touch my head, but I jerked away and an awkwardness fell between us. She noticed some of my drawings on the ground by her foot.

"I didn't realize how good you got at drawing." She picked up my drawing pad. "You know, with me being gone all the time…" Her head tilted as she studied the picture I'd drew of Lev. "Who is this?" I immediately grabbed the notepad from her hands, afraid the prints from Rita's camera would slip out.

"It's no one."

I hopped out of bed. She took a deep breath.

"I don't want you to have the same life I had, Mae. That's why I'm doing this," she said, turning to me. "I had a hard time in school, just like you, because of how my mother raised me. She would fill my head with stories and myths from the past. She taught me and your aunt at home before I went to school, like Grandpa taught you. Dad thought her stories were nonsense back then. When I finally started school, I quickly learned that my ideas of the world were backwards compared to what I learned at home. I was behind in my education, and it felt humiliating. Dad was furious with my mother, blaming her for my issues in school. He was able to repair the damage, and I was able to go to Lukenic. Dad didn't believe in all that stuff she used to teach us. But after she died, that all changed."

"What are you trying to tell me?" I asked.

"Going to Lukenic helped me get back on the right track. I know you aren't exactly going to the same program as I did, but I trust them with your education. I know you will grow into a healthy adult by doing this, Mae." She paused, steeling herself to go deeper. "I didn't realize how much my mother's death affected my father and his thinking.

It made him question everything, especially the Abnormal. I thought it would be okay for him to raise you while your dad and I worked for a while, but I guess Mom's death took a bigger toll on him that I realized." As she finished, she looked like she wanted to cry, but no tears came.

"It won't be too bad. Remember, Dad and I both graduated from Lukenic. It seems scary, but you will make lots of friends. I wish you would just be attending there like an ordinary student. Just remember that regardless of what Grandpa taught you, you are a very bright kid, Mae. Even if the test scores doesn't show it, or your teachers don't see it. Even though you think I don't see it, I do. And Rita will be nearby. I'm sure you will get a chance to see her."

Part of me had forgotten about Rita being at the same school as me now. I wished I could be excited, but it seemed like our friendship wouldn't be the same anymore. Ms. Vivly said that I wouldn't be in the same part of campus as the actual Lukenic students. Mom sat there with me for a bit, trying to make me feel like this was the best thing for me. It wasn't long before I got up and gathered my stuff. I didn't want to be in my mother's presence. The story of her relationship with her parents didn't change anything. She hadn't told me anything I couldn't have guessed.

Lukenic appeared among the trees, surrounded by big, beautiful homes. The car ride was silent. As my parents and I approached the large campus, we saw a black iron fence surrounding the school. "Welcome to Lukenic," a black metal sign with gold letters read. We drove past it, heading through the entrance gate. There were students in their uniforms walking around or sitting in the grass studying.

In the middle of the campus was a pearl-white building made of stone that overshadowed the entire neighborhood. It towered over the campus like the master of all knowledge of time and space, logic and nature, mathematics and science, good and evil. There was a large overhang held up by four large pillars, that looked like they were holding open Lukenic's mouth. Although it wasn't smiling, the school seemed to bring happiness to everyone else. It was quite an achievement in a young student's career to be accepted here.

We finally reached the entrance for students like me. It was on the opposite end of the main gate. As we pulled up, I hardly saw anyone, only a gardener outside the building raking leaves. Unlike on the other side of campus, I saw no students. Dad parked in front of a tall brick building. It looked old, almost abandoned. A lot of overgrown trees dominated the area.

"Is this the right place?" Mom asked. I sank in my seat, knowing this was it. Given my family's reputation here, I felt like a disappointment since I wasn't there for the same reason the other students were accepted. Dad pulled out the pamphlet Ms. Vivly had given him, looking at the campus's map. "She said it was the old humanities building, and according to this map, this is the correct place," Dad said as he got out of the car.

All the windows of the building were dark, like something was covering them from the inside. What were they trying to hide?

"I don't think this place was running when I was in school," Mom said, looking back at me. Some of the other buildings in the area were boarded shut. "I understand you're angry with us, but anything you need, you just tell us, okay?"

"Can you have Marty contact me as soon as possible?" I replied, keeping my eyes averted.

She took a deep breath, turned back, and sank into her seat. "Sure."

I opened the car door, stepped out, and leaned against the car. I looked toward a brick wall that separated this campus from the real one. Vines and barbed wire covered the top. It was silent on my side, with just a faint sound of students from the other side.

"This is the place," Dad said, coming out of the building. I followed my parents inside, and we entered a spacious, empty entrance hall. The floor looked like it had been shiny once but was now muted and flat. A staircase stood in front of us, zigzagging its way up. The smell wasn't unpleasant, but the scent was like an old house. A woman came from around the corner from a room to the left. She walked over to us, smiling.

"Hello. Welcome to Lukenic's rehabilitation program. I'm Ms. Lowkuss."

"Thank you," Mom replied. "I'm Elliana, and this is my daughter, Mae." I gave a faint smile and looked away.

"Welcome, Mae," Ms. Lowkuss said. "I know you will learn a lot during your stay here."

I looked down the hall from where she came. It seemed like she was the only person here.

"Where are the other students?" I asked.

"Well, most of them are here, just in their rooms, and your roommate is here, too. I can introduce you to her."

She took us up to the fifth floor, where I would be staying. As we climbed the stairs, she explained what each level was for. The second floor was where we took our classes. The third was where we ate, and the fourth was where the boys slept. The fifth was for girls. We came to the room where I was staying. It was tiny, with just enough space for the things already inside. There was a bed on each side of the room with one desk, a light, and a drawer beside each bed.

"Avery, you have guests. Your new roommate is here!" To the

left of the room, a girl was lying on the bed against the wall with her back to us. Her long blond hair draped from the bed to the floor. She moved slowly, rolling toward us, then sat up from the bed. She looked drowsy, and most of her mask had peeled off her left cheek, revealing her Abnormal underneath. "Oh, my," Ms. Lowkuss said, rushing over to Avery to fix her mask.

"Don't touch me," Avery said, brushing Ms. Lowkuss off harshly.

"I'm just trying to help you, Avery," Ms. Lowkuss said. "You have guests. You don't want them to see you like this, do you?"

"I don't care," Avery snapped back. I could tell the mask Avery wore was one of the most expensive kinds. It was disposable, the liquid variety that came in a tub. You applied it like facial cream and, within minutes, you had new skin. You peeled it off when you were done with it.

"Okay, well, this is Avery. Don't mind her. Everyone here needs a lot of work, but we will take care of that."

Avery glared at me, and I quickly looked away from her. Folded neatly on my bed was my uniform. Mom walked over and sat on my mattress, holding up pieces of my uniform. A dark gray blazer, black sweater vest, black tie, five gray skirts, five white blouses, and five black stockings.

"Looks like the Lukenic uniform hasn't changed," Mom said. Dad brought my things to my bed, and I came to sit next to Mom. She pulled me close to her, holding me and kissing my head to comfort me, but I felt nothing. It seemed like a bad dream I was waiting to wake up from.

Avery was fully awake by the time Dad finished up the paperwork and my parents left. She sat up with her back against the headboard and her knees pulled against her chest. She stared out the window between our beds. She was older than me, maybe sixteen or seventeen.

Avery was what everyone in Eradeem would consider a beautiful girl, at least with her mask on. She was tall and thin, with long blond hair and fair skin. But it wasn't long before she started picking at her cheek where the mask was torn.

"I hope you don't mind," Avery said nonchalantly as she dropped pieces of her mask onto the bed. There was a mirror in our room, but she stayed where she was. This was clearly more of a bad habit than a hygienic practice. "Actually, I don't care if you do mind; you're just going to have to get over it," she said before I could say anything.

I sat on the edge of the bed, tucking my arms to my belly.

"I don't mind," I replied, trying not to look at her. From one side of her cheek to the other, she had removed the mask from her face. The dark veins of her Abnormal ended on the lower part of her face and reached under her clothes. She peeled the skin from her neck.

"I never knew anyone who didn't wear a mask in front of people," I said.

"Good for you. Why are you here?" Avery sneered and turned to me.

"I'm not sure. I guess it's because of my grades."

"Grades!?" Avery chuckled. "What else? They don't just send you here for grades. There are other places for that." She got up from her bed, grabbed the chair from the desk, and sat on it backward, scooting close to me. She rested her chin over her folded arms on the top of the chair.

"Tell me something juicy. I know you're hiding something. Did you get in a dirty fight?" I shifted farther back on the bed. She was so close, I could almost feel her breathing. Avery kept her eyes on me, smiling. "Is it my face?" she asked, nodding. "Does it make you uncomfortable?" she said, tilting her head.

"No, of course not," I lied, looking away. She had power in her

Abnormal. She knew it made people distressed. I guessed it was her way to have some control over others.

"You can probably tell I don't have friends, but I don't want friends. And just because we're roommates doesn't mean we are friends."

"Okay," I said, glancing at her.

"So, why are you really here?" I wasn't sure what I should tell her. That I had too much exposure to my crazy star-chasing grandfather? I didn't want to sound weak, but I didn't want to give myself away, either.

"Or did the baby not use her mask properly?" Avery laughed, pulling closer to me.

"For leaving Eradeem." The words crept out of my mouth, and I immediately regretted them. Avery pulled back from me.

"Leaving Eradeem?" she said, erupting with laughter. "That's the dumbest thing I ever heard! How do you do that?"

"Um, you know," I started, trying to fix my answer. "I just went through the woods, and then I got caught. At the border," I slowly explained.

Avery just stared for a moment. "Really?"

"Yes."

"I don't believe you."

Good, I thought to myself.

"That makes no sense. How can you leave Eradeem? Wouldn't you fall off or something?"

"I don't know, but I got caught, so there is nothing else to say." It didn't occur to me until then that there wasn't a concept for leaving Eradeem. Eradeem was the world, so how could you leave it?

"You must be here for delusions or something. You sound like those homeless people."

"So, what about you?" I asked.

"I'm not afraid to take my mask off in front of people, especially in school. People think it's strange. They think I must have some psychological problem. But I don't."

"That's pretty brave," I said. Avery raised her brow, then glared at me.

"It is?"

"Yeah, of course. I mean that you don't care what people think of you. I think that's brave."

"Well, the truth is, I don't think my Abnormal is ugly," Avery said, turning toward the mirror and smiling. "I'm hoping one day it covers my whole body until I'm like a monster. They're my beauty marks. I feel like a monster on the inside, so it should match."

"Who can say you are wrong? Maybe you're right, and everyone else is wrong?" I said. Avery stopped smiling and slowly pushed herself away from me again. Her eyes narrowed.

"You're pretty strange, Mae. That's your name, right?" She stared at me like my teachers and classmates used to do when I first started school.

"Yes, that's my name."

"What's with your mom?" Avery asked. "She must be covered in Abnormal."

"What do you mean?" I said.

"I guess you're used to seeing your mom with a mask caked on like that, and who wears long sleeves in this weather?"

"Yeah, I guess you're right."

"Well, Mae, my new roommate, I like you. I think we're going to be good friends. Take that as a compliment, because I don't like most people."

Fourteen

I wasn't sure what to expect the next day as a Lukenic student *reject*. I learned that Avery and I would be in the same class, even though she was at least three years older than me. We were never told what kind of class it was, just that it started at seven a.m. I thought I would have seen more students the previous day, but I'd only met Avery.

It must be a small program, because besides Avery and me, there were only three other students in our class that morning. Looking at the group, I stopped short. I recognized one of the students: it was Fane. The guy I'd met just a few months before was sitting in the second row, right behind the desk labelled as mine. Avery sat to his left as I slowly walked in behind her. Fane looked up from his desk at me, but I looked away.

I tried my best not to seem awkward as I sat before him and between the other two students. The boy to my left was much younger than I was. He looked like he was about ten. His thick black hair reminded me of what Dad might have looked like when he was younger, but with big hazel eyes. The name on his desk read "Dime."

To my other side, a boy rubbed his nails repeatedly against his desk as his knee bounced. He had wavy brown hair that dangled over his face, and his tag said "Theo." He was around Avery and Fane's age. I caught his dark blue eyes looking at me, then away. He seemed irritable. I watched the door for more students, but none ever came.

"Mae, right?" Fane said, breaking the silence in the room. I turned around in my seat, trying to hide my dullness. He was just as handsome as I had remembered. He smiled back at me, which didn't help my nervousness. I was glad my skin wasn't light, so my feelings wouldn't be exposed. I usually wasn't afraid of anything except for older, attractive boys.

"So, we meet again." Fane smiled, leaned forward, and rested his chin on his palm.

"Yeah," I replied with a slight chuckle. I wanted to say something else, but nothing came out.

"So, I guess you aren't here because of your smart parents."

"I guess not," I said, pausing, trying to think of something clever. "I'm just here." I felt a little sick having to play it cool.

"Okay, that's good. The first step to recovery is getting here."

"Right," I said back. It was hard to look at him, he was so pretty. His smile didn't help. I turned around, trying to keep my face in order.

"Who's your friend, Mae?" Avery jumped in. She was leaning back in her seat, watching us both, her arms crossed under her chest. She looked slightly shocked at me. She was wearing her mask today, and I could tell she was happy she was.

"Well, he—" I started, but then I was cut off.

"It's a nobody. Just a pain," Theo said, not even looking over at us, only straight ahead.

"My name is Fane," he replied, letting out a long sigh. "Don't mind him. Some people have a hard time making friends."

"Oh really!" Theo pushed his desk forward and jumped up from his seat as he looked at Fane. "Say that to my face."

Fane didn't move. He stayed in his seat, glaring up at Theo. "Sit down before I have to make you. Don't embarrass yourself."

"Make me sit down, then!" Theo shouted. Fane turned away from Theo, calmly looking back at Avery. "And what is your name?"

"A-ver-y," she said slowly. She seemed to be bracing herself as she looked at Theo.

"Don't worry; he won't do anything," Fane said. But before Fane could continue talking, Theo pushed his desk over and charged toward him. Fane stood quickly, so Theo missed when he took a swing at him. Then Theo's face was suddenly smacked down on the desk with Fane's hand pressed on his head. Fane had Theo's arm twisted behind his back while Theo's other arm tried pushing himself up. It happened so fast I didn't have time to react or move out of the way.

"They've been fighting since yesterday," Dime said, glancing back at them. Theo couldn't even struggle, and his whole body was red now.

"Let me go," Theo shouted.

"You promise you'll be a good boy, Theo?" Fane mocked.

"Get off me!" Theo yelled. Fane let him go, and Theo jumped up from the desk. He grabbed his shoulder as he slowly picked up his chair, but not without spewing some insults.

"I think I'm going to enjoy my time here," Avery said, throwing her hands behind her head and grinning.

Not long after the fight, our professor entered the room, and my eyebrow twitched. It was Mr. Owns. He walked in front of the class with the same black suit and tiny-tented glasses as before. He came off as more of a bodyguard than a teacher. He said nothing, but our class quickly came to order in his presence. He walked over to the board and began writing "Collective, Conscious, Social, Order" on the board, vertically. Beside each word, he wrote its definition.

Collective: Involving all members of a group.

Conscious: The awareness of self.

Social: Relating to society in general.

Order: An authoritative command or instruction.

He turned to the class with his hands behind him. "Before we get into our lesson, I am going to lay down the rules." His voice was deep and raspy, and it was a bit weird hearing him for the first time when it was the third time I had seen him.

"While here, you are not to leave campus or even this section of campus. After our lessons, you are allowed two hours of free time. After that, you will be sent to your rooms. Lights-out is at eight p.m. You are not to be in each other's rooms, and there is no speaking to other students not in this program. If anyone from the other side is on this part of campus, you ignore them. On the board is the new course of study that we will focus on while you are here in this rehabilitation program at Lukenic." He paced back and forth across the front of the room. "Collective Conscious and Social Order is what this course is called. I have already given you the meaning of each word.

"Now I want you to write down what this class will be about and why it applies to you being here." He handed out pens and papers to each of us and then sat at his desk. He kept his eyes on us the whole time as we wrote, so I tried my best to look focused. I simply wrote what I knew they wanted me to. This class is to make us like the other normal students. I wasn't sure at the time what everyone else in class had done to be sent here, other than Avery, but I was sure it had something to do with continual disruption in class, or society. There wasn't much to learn in our time here. It started to feel like this place was made to keep us away from other people until we learned to follow along with what was expected of us.

Regardless of how I acted, I truly wanted to be like everyone else. Yet, knowing that not even the kids here believed I had left Eradeem, I wasn't so sure I could ever be normal. Maybe if Grandpa wasn't in my life, I would be a different person. Maybe I would be more like everyone else—not giving such childish fantasies the time of day. Maybe the things people my age were consumed by would consume me, too, instead of my grandfather's research. Rita being at this school was the only thing that kept me from going into a deep sadness; but it seemed like she would never know I was here. I completed my paper and turned it in to Mr. Owns. We spent the rest of our time that day trying not to fall asleep to a series of videos on assimilation.

When it was over, we were released. Avery was the first to leave the class. I wanted to follow her, but she was too fast. It seemed she didn't really want to do free time with us. I figured I could meet up with her later, so instead I found Theo and Dime sitting outside the courtyard. Theo was lying against a large stone that Dime was sitting on, but Fane was nowhere around.

"Mae!" Theo called out to me, waving his hand. I walked over, taking a seat on the grass.

"So, how are you liking this place?" Theo asked with a straight face, knowing the answer.

"I don't," I replied. "I'm just trying to be good so I can leave."

"Well, there is definitely not a way to leave I already tried. They have a gate blocking us off from the other students, and security at all the exits."

"That sucks," I replied. "I really was hoping to go to the other side of campus. My best friend just started there. She probably doesn't know I'm here; though."

"Well, so much for you trying to be good," Theo said, air-quoting the word good. "I never saw you here at Lukenic before. You must have come from a different school."

"I used to go to Charper." Both of their eyebrows wrinkled. "But both of my parents were students here, and so was my grandfather."

"So this is your first time at Lukenic?"

"Yeah, but I'm not a Lukenic student."

"So, you have the connections to get in Lukenic, just not in the way you were hoping," Theo said.

"Right, I guess you could say that."

"Lucky for you. Normally kids outside of Lukenic are taken somewhere much worse for their behavior."

"Really?"

"So where is your friend Avery? You should bring her over here with us."

"I don't know where she is."

Theo seemed very different now that he wasn't inside. He'd untucked his shirt, unbuttoned a few buttons, and rolled his sleeves. Our uniforms were to be always worn neatly. Our uniforms had to be pressed, with clean shoes. But there wasn't anyone out here to watch us, other than a few security guards at the entry. I didn't think, anyway. It was hard to trust that we were ever left alone.

"Figures. She's always off somewhere."

"Did you guys already know each other?" I asked.

"Ahh, well, not really. She's been at Lukenic as long as me," Theo said. "Because we're the same age, almost all our classes were together, but we barely talked."

"So, all of you guys were already students at Lukenic before coming here?"

"Well, still students at Lukenic. This is their reform program," answered Theo.

"So why are you guys here?"

Theo took a deep breath. "My dad put me in this program because I can't control my anger. He couldn't handle the negative feedback my professors were giving him. Everyone knew I was causing problems, and it brought big shame on him."

"So you were that out of control?" I asked.

Theo chuckled. "It doesn't really take much to be considered out of control at Lukenic; but compared to most people, I guess I am. My dad's a judge, so it doesn't look good for his reputation to have me around other students who might tell their parents about me." He lay down in the grass, kicking up his leg over his knee, watching the sky. "But I couldn't care less."

"How about you?" I said, looking at Dime, but he quickly turned away.

"He won't talk about it. I already asked him."

It was kind of strange to see a teenage guy hanging around this little kid. But I guessed Theo's hatred of Fane was very real, and who else was there to spend time with? Theo looked like an older brother hanging around Dime.

"So, tell us why you are here, Mae."

"Well..." I said, hesitating. "Trespassing."

"Trespassing?" Theo said, sitting up to look at me. "Really, trespassing?" He chuckled as he lay back down.

"Where, on a military base?"

"Um...something like that. Do you know about Fane? Why he's here?" I asked, trying to change the subject.

"Who knows, who cares? I never seen that guy here before."

"Really?" I replied. "I met him a few months ago. He was in the Lukenic uniform just walking around near my bus stop."

"Bus stop?" Theo chuckled. "You really are an outsider. Anyways, I don't know the guy. And I don't wanna know him."

"If you don't know him, what happened? School just started and you both are fighting?"

"I didn't start anything. That guy is a jerk. He came in our dorm like he owned everything, trying to tell me where I would sleep and what I could have in the room. He came in disrespecting us, like he ran the place. Right, Dime?"

"He is a bit overbearing, I suppose," Dime replied.

"A bit overbearing— that's an understatement! I had to put him in his place. And that's that."

"Really," I said. "He seems pretty nice to me."

"You're a girl, of course he'll be nice to you; but get too close and I'm sure you'll see."

Fifteen

The days at Lukenic were all the same. We were lectured every day on the importance of assimilating into society. We were shown how to look for those who led as examples and how to follow their behavior. Copying whatever the majority of people did was the way to survive in a society. We wrote papers on how we would handle certain situations the right way and the wrong way; and, at the end of each day, we'd watch some video on what we'd just learned. After about a month, the class seemed to start all over, and we relearned the same things again, in the same order.

I found myself with Theo and Dime most of the time during our breaks. Dime seemed to just be there, hardly ever talking. He was very mature and articulate. Sometimes I would forget that he was only ten years old, but then sometimes he looked like he wanted to cry. Theo was fidgety in class mostly; it seemed like he had a hard time focusing.

Several times he was told to leave the class if Mr. Owns thought he was distracting the rest of us. Like if he was sighing too much, or grunting, or talking to himself quietly. When that happened, Ms. Lowkuss would come and take him somewhere. Theo wouldn't say where. After about twenty minutes, he would come back relaxed, but almost too relaxed. He would move more slowly, be more serious, and seem a bit irritated by us. If he had a day like that, then he would just go off alone during breaks. One day when Ms. Lowkuss came for him, he exploded. "I'm fine!" he yelled, slamming his fist on his desk.

"No, you're not," Mr. Owns replied, grabbing Theo by the collar and pulling him up from his seat, almost tossing him to Ms. Lowkuss. He pushed Ms. Lowkuss away when she tried to grab him, and Mr. Owns immediately restrained him until security came. Whatever they were doing with him, I could tell that it was bad. Theo started to try his best to act accordingly so he didn't have to leave.

After class, Avery always disappeared. I would ask her where she went, but she wouldn't tell me. Fane usually stayed around the campus, roaming and not bothering anybody. I didn't think Fane seemed as bad as Theo tried to make him out to be. One day after class, he handed me a note saying to meet him at the old running track over to the side of our building toward the end of our break.

It was about an hour before curfew when I made my way to meet up with Fane. The old track looked like it hadn't been touched in decades. The grass was overgrown, and the bleachers were rusty and creaky. Signs were faded so that you couldn't read them, and the concrete concession stand was conquered by vines. Grass grew through the cracks of the sidewalk. I didn't notice Fane at first until he called my name. He looked down at me from the top of the bleachers.

"Are you looking for me?" he called. He waved with his usual handsome smile.

"I never noticed this place," I said, looking around. I made my way up the bleachers to join him. "Are we allowed here?"

"Of course we are. This place isn't locked away. And security passes here every so often. So, it's open for us."

I was a little hesitant because we were both alone. "I have a good view of the city from here," Fane said, smiling. As I sat next to him, he asked, "Did I scare you?"

"No, not really," I replied. I kept my hands snugged between my legs, facing upward, trying not to look at him. It was more uncomfortable sitting next to him than walking around the abandoned campus alone.

"Are you okay?" Fane asked, trying to look me in the eye. I kept reaching toward the back of my neck, pulling on my hair and pushing it back over my ear. I'm sure it was painful to watch; I only hoped it wasn't obvious how strange I was acting.

"Yes." I smiled, forcing my hands down to my lap. "I am fine. It's just a little cold out here."

"Here," Fane said, pulling off his school jacket and placing it on my shoulders. "Better?"

His scent surrounded me.

"Yes, it's better. Thanks."

I felt so stupid blaming the weather for my nervousness, but I was happy to take his jacket. I didn't actually feel cold, but the warmth of the fabric felt so comfortable. I thought that if a boy gave you his jacket to wear, it was because he liked you. Like more than a friend. But Fane and I weren't even friends, so I wasn't sure what I was supposed to think. Why had he called me out here alone?

"So, what do you think?" Fane asked me.

I was lost in the moment, so I wasn't sure what to say. What did I think of what? Did he really like me? I felt my cheeks getting warm at the thought. I was thinking that maybe he just saw me as a kid, since I was younger than he was.

"I think you are really sweet," I replied.

"What do you mean?" Fane said, quirking his brow. And then I realized he was talking about something else.

"Umm?"

Fane chuckled. "I meant the view."

"Oh," I replied. "Of course, the view."

Convincing myself it was an honest mistake. Right before us was the metropolis of Eradeem: tall buildings that lit up the sky, surrounded by red clouds. They were always very thick in that part of Eradeem, but as the sky stretched away from the city, the clouds were thinner. We could see the sun setting as some of its light pierced through the clouds.

It reminded me of what Eradeem looked like from the outside—like a spot against the more beautiful nature.

"You know why I asked you to come out here with me?"

"Why?"

"You're the only one here who seems to actually be normal. I just really need that in my life after being put in this program."

"Really?"

"Of course. In class, they said to surround yourself with people like you. Well-behaved, follows directions. I know you're much younger than me, but I want to get better and progress out of this program."

"Oh, you think that I'm good?"

"I've been watching you, and out of everyone, you seem to be the one who will graduate the soonest."

"You think so?" I asked.

"Yes, you're completely different from Avery. She is definitely a troublemaker. You can tell how she carries herself; and she never comes out during free time, just keeps away in her room."

"Oh, well… Yeah…I'm not sure where she goes during free time."

"Is she not usually in her room?"

"Well, no."

"That's what I mean, she always seems like she's up to no good, unlike you. It's important to share what's going on with her, so she can get better. She is your friend."

"This is a really good view," I said, changing the subject. Maybe I shared too much about Avery.

"Yes, I think so. It's pretty stunning."

I glanced at him as he watched the sunset. I wondered what his story was. He didn't really seem like the kind of person who needed to be here.

"Fane?" I asked. "Do you ever think about there being something more than what you can see?" Sitting there watching the city helped my mind sober to the reality about Eradeem. I didn't know if Lev's story was the truth. All I knew was what I had seen outside of Eradeem.

"What do you mean?" Fane said, sounding a bit confused.

"I mean, you can see the clouds, the buildings, and everything you know of. You ever wonder if there are more things to see? What if there are things you don't know?"

"Yes, I'm sure there are things we don't know about; but it's the scientists' job to worry about that, so there's no need to wonder."

"What if someone did know more? But they won't share it with us?"

"Like who?"

"Anyone."

"I don't know," Fane said as he leaned back, resting his elbows on the seat behind him. "That would suck, I guess. But if they were to hide something important from us, it's probably for our own good."

For our own good? I thought. But why would it be for our own good? The military had to know something if they had a wall surrounding Eradeem. I wondered what Marty knew.

"You think about a lot of things, Mae. I bet that's why you're here, huh?" Fane said.

"Oh," I replied as I moved Fane's jacket from my shoulders and slid my arms into it to wear it. As it got darker, it became colder.

"So, why are you here?" I asked Fane. He took a deep breath, pausing before saying anything.

"I prefer to keep why I'm here to myself."

Moments later, the red lights in the city cut out, replacing the daylight. Curfew was ending, so we left that place and headed into our dorms. I returned Fane's jacket as we parted in the hall. Fane went to his floor, and I went to mine. I dropped straight into my bed, falling to my face to collect my feelings, replaying my foolish moment. I felt happy for the time I spent with him, hoping we could get another chance to hang out. I almost convinced myself that he could be interested in me but then, what if he was? What was I going to do with a boyfriend, especially in this program?

I looked over at the clock, and it was five minutes before curfew was over, and Avery hadn't returned yet. Ms. Lowkuss usually would come around this time to check that we were in our rooms. I didn't know the consequences for being late for curfew, but I had a feeling I might be about to find out.

The door opened, and Ms. Lowkuss entered like she did every

night. I panicked, because Avery still wasn't here.

"Hello, Mae."

"Hi," I replied, looking over at Avery's empty bed.

Ms. Lowkuss followed my gaze and turned back to me. "Where is Avery?"

"Well, she is—" But before I could answer, Avery came in behind Ms. Lowkuss, pushing through the door.

"Bathroom, I was in the bathroom, Ms. Lowkuss."

"The bathroom? You could have waited until I did my regular check-in."

"Well, I'm sorry, but it was an emergency, and I had to go now. I'm sorry for that. Won't happen again."

"Let's hope so. You are now free to go to the restroom," Ms. Lowkuss said as she left our room.

"That was close, Avery. What happened?" Avery flopped down on the end of her bed, pulling off her socks, shoes, and then mask.

"I was with my friends," Avery said. She popped up suddenly from her bed, looking at me like she'd made a mistake.

"Your friends?" I replied.

Avery chuckled, tightening her smile. "Yeah, my friends! I know more people than just you, you know." She lay back down on her bed, kicking her foot up against the wall. "But it doesn't really matter that you know; my sister wants to meet you. I told her I would bring you one day."

"What?" I replied. "Where?"

"On the other side of campus. Where the normal people sleep."

"Wait, you've been going over there this whole time? Why didn't you tell me?"

"Yeah," she said and shrugged.

"My best friend is over there, Avery; I have to talk to her. Will you really take me over there?”

“I just said I was going to bring you.”

“Well, can you help me find her?” I pleaded.

“We won’t have time for that. Do you know how many students are over there? You better just hope you run into her.”

I knew it was against the rules to leave, but I really had to talk to Rita. Her mother was keeping me from her, so this was my opportunity to talk to her in depth about that night. I didn’t have the pictures with me, but if she had her camera, she could see the photos I had taken that night.

“So, you said your sister wants to meet me?”

“Yeah, she’s the more acceptable version of me. I told her about you getting caught in the woods and that your grandfather is Niles Cefend.”

“What?” I said. “How do you know who my grandfather is?”

“I overheard Fane talking about you with Ms. Lowkuss. I don’t know why you kept it a secret...but anyways, we can go tomorrow, if you don’t have any plans, which I’m sure you don’t.”

“Of course not. But wait, why would your sister care about my grandpa?”

“Well, I guess you can say she’s a big fan of his.”

Sixteen

All I could think about was going to the other side of campus. I hardly paid any attention in class, but it didn't make much of difference. Having something to look forward to gave me a break from all the social resetting being done to me.

I was excited to maybe see Rita—but I was also curious about Avery and her sister. Who was this person who was a fan of Grandpa? Grandpa's peak in popularity was before I was born, so it was hard to imagine anyone my age who looked up to him. Even though Avery didn't want to help me find Rita, I was sure her sister would be helpful. I had no idea how Avery got any access to the other side, but if I had to befriend her sister to get that privilege, I was more than happy to do so. I wondered if Rita knew I was here. I was sure she would be shocked to see me. But both she and I knew I couldn't be at Lukenic because of my good behavior.

I was supposed to meet Avery near one of the old buildings

without being noticed. When class ended, Ms. Lowkuss came in the room, asking me to follow her to the main hall on the first floor. I was a bit surprised that I was suddenly being summoned. I looked at Avery as I left the room. She gave me a questioning look, and I only shrugged.

"Is there something wrong, Ms. Lowkuss?"

"Oh no. You just have a visitor."

"I do? Who?"

"I believe it's a cousin of yours."

I followed Ms. Lowkuss to the bottom of the staircase, where I saw Marty in his military uniform standing near the entrance. I ran down the stairs into his arms, holding him tight. I had never been away from my family for so long. Marty picked me up and swung me in the air. Seeing him was like seeing a ghost. It had been over a month, and I hadn't heard from anyone.

"Are you an angel?" I chuckled as he put me down. I touched his face, testing if he was a dream.

"Now you're overdoing it, Mae." Marty smiled. I got permission to go outside with Marty, but only for fifteen minutes.

"You don't know how good it is to see you. This place is horrible," I said, hugging his arm. I didn't want to let go. I thought when he left, he could take a part of me with him.

"I miss you, too, Mae, but you got yourself into this mess, you know."

We found a stone bench to sit down on. I released his arm, remembering why I was here.

"So, I guess you were the one who told on me?" I frowned, looking down at my feet.

"I had no choice, Mae. The next day my boss came to me and asked about the incident. I couldn't lie and say you were never there.

The other officer saw you. You shouldn't have been out there anyway." I didn't have anything to say in my defense. They'd placed me in a prison designed to look like a school as a punishment. I could say I regretted it, but I wasn't so sure I did.

"So, are you at least making any friends?"

"It's a prison for kids," I replied, making Marty burst into laughter.

"It's just a place to help you become a better person. If it were a prison, they wouldn't let me come or let you out so we could have this conversation."

"I'm technically still inside, Marty."

"It can't be too bad. As soon as you start acting like a model student, you'll be out of here in no time."

"Sure," I said, wanting to change the subject. "How's Aunt and Uncle?"

"They're fine. Dad is hardly home, as usual, and Mom is just trying to handle being alone since I started working more hours."

"And Marcella?" I asked. Marty let out a deep sigh.

"She's still going through Pains."

"Oh." Marty's expression had changed slightly. "It must be bad."

"I think it's getting worse."

"So do the doctors know what's going on?"

"They just keep saying that it should have passed. She should have stopped having Pains more than a month ago. It's hard watching a baby go through this. I just wish someone could do something, or that I could make it stop."

"I wish I could see her. I miss holding her." I looked down at my hands, imagining her being in my arms. "I'd rather be there with her than here."

"So, have you seen Rita here yet?"

"No, we aren't allowed on that part of campus, or to talk to the

142

other students."

"Oh, well, that sucks."

"Yeah," I said. "So, have you heard anything from Grandpa yet?"

He shot me a glance. "You're still on that, Mae?"

"Yes, he's my grandpa. I want to know if he's okay. You said that you were going to be working at the prison. Why is it so bad that I want to know if he's fine?"

"Sorry," he said pulling me close to his side for a small forgive-me hug. "It's just that…" He paused and sighed. "Never mind."

"No, tell me."

"Look, Grandpa is fine. And I did get a chance to see him."

"Really?" I said, almost jumping from my seat. "So?"

"So what?"

"Did you get to talk to him?"

"Not really. I saw him from his cell. We didn't talk."

"So, when can I go visit him?"

"Visit?" Marty snapped. "Are you crazy?"

"You said that you would help me see him."

"Well, I changed my mind."

"Marty, please, it's of the utmost importance that I see him."

"Why?" Marty asked. "What is so important that I must risk my position to let a little girl talk to a prisoner? It's because of him you're here, remember that. He filled your head with all those childish fantasies. And now you're here so that they can fix the damage done to you."

People said these things often to me, but it was harder to hear from someone I loved. My family all knew this about Grandpa, but no one ever talked about it. They didn't like dragging Grandpa's name through the dirt, even if it was already dirty. Nothing he said was new to me, but I was heartbroken to hear it.

"He's not crazy," I said, trying not to yell.

"Mae, please just let it go."

"No!" I snapped. I wiped the tears from my eyes before they let loose. "I'll tell you why I must see him, but you have to promise me you'll let me if I do. And that you will not share what I'm going to tell you with anyone."

Marty pulled back as his eyes searched my face. "Okay?" he said, sounding unsure.

"It's about why you found me by the wall that night. And probably why Grandpa is in jail."

"So what happened?" Marty said, glaring at me.

"Promise me first," I demanded.

"I can't promise you anything, Mae. Tell me, and I'll decide if it's worth helping you."

"Then just promise you won't tell anyone what I am going to tell you."

"Fine, I promise."

I was so desperate to see Grandpa that I was willing to sound crazy in front of Marty. I needed to know why Grandpa had been going out at night every Friday.

I took a deep breath, then started.

"The night I was missing after Grandpa was arrested, I was on the other side of the border, beyond the desert."

Marty's eyes narrowed, but I continued.

"I made a plan to go out in the woods to his base to search for clues, since no one would tell me what happened to him. When I got to his base, these strange lights were floating in the sky, and one of them came to me. So, I followed where the rest were coming from by going beyond Grandpa's base; and somehow, I was on the other side. I don't know how, but it was like magic. I wondered if maybe the thing

I found could be the reason for his arrest."

Marty was silent for a bit. He knew I wasn't someone to lie about things, but I couldn't tell if he believed me or not. I only hoped he would let me see Grandpa.

"Okay, well…" Marty finally started. "That's a story."

"I know it sounds crazy."

"Yes, it does, but it might be good that you see him."

"Really?" I said, jumping up, but then paused. "Wait, why do you say it like that?"

"Look, just be happy that I'm going to help you. I'll come back in a few days and work something out to take you to him."

Seventeen

Avery told me to meet her in the back end of the campus yard behind a building, which was surprisingly close to our quarters, where there was a small storage shack with the windows boarded up. We had to go there at separate times to avoid bringing attention to what we were doing. I had to be sure no one was watching me before I disappeared behind the shack. Avery was already there, leaning against the shed, facing the fence. She was wearing a dark blue hoodie over her uniform.

Part of the fence behind the shack was overtaken by the bushes from the other side. The woods were so thick that it almost looked like part of the fence was invisible. The other part had barbed wire on top that blocked us from going over it.

"This fence is parallel to the other side of campus."

"So, how are we going to go through it?" I asked.

"Don't worry, there's an opening. It's been there since I was a kid.

I used to come over to this part of Lukenic all the time before they made it my punishment, but I'm pretty sure no one else knows about it."

Avery vanished through the metal and leaves.

"Come!" she said as her hand appeared through the bushes, signaling me to step in. As I approached, Avery took my hand, pulling me through as I ducked my head down to met her. She poked her head back out to be sure no one was watching us before she led me to the other side. The woods were so thick that it was hard to tell if we were even going the right way. But it didn't take Avery much time to find her way to a man-made path; I assumed Avery had made it.

"I think you'll like my sister. She's much nicer than me," Avery said.

"So why does she want to see me, again?" I asked.

"I don't know. I just told her that you got caught trying to leave Eradeem and mentioned who your grandpa was."

"It's just weird. Most people make fun of Grandpa."

"You mean people like me?" Avery chuckled. "My sister is a little weird."

"Weirder than you?" I asked.

"Um, no, but in her own way."

I started to hear the sound of people chatting and walking against the pavement the closer we got.

"We're almost there," Avery said. "We just have to be sure no one notices us. Well, that no one notices me. No one knows who you are, so you should be fine." We finally reached the other side where the gate was broken open. Avery peeked through and waited a moment until it was clear.

"Okay, let's go." She took my hand, and we both moved out of the woods to the campus. Avery pulled the hood of her jacket over her head as we got to the center of the campus, where most of the students were.

Lukenic was very different from this side, though I was surprised to note that there were even more security guards here. Every building was bustling with students moving in and out. The students were very beautiful. They were all wearing top-of-the-line masks like Avery, Theo, and Fane wore. I wanted to take in everything. But I kept my eyes focused on the students so that I'd see Rita if she passed. We reached the dorms. Students pulled out cards, swiping them against a pad to get in.

Avery quickly followed behind the nearest person going inside the dorm, and I stayed close by. When we were inside, we walked up three flights of stairs past girls coming up and down. Some were in their casual clothes; others were still in their uniforms. Some girls were older, and some were younger. I scanned around the heads of girls below me as we moved up the stairs, then stopped to get a better look. Avery saw that I wasn't following her, so she grabbed my hand, snapping my focus back to her. Once we were on the third floor, she walked up to one of the doors. She looked around before she entered, pulling me in along with her. We walked into what looked like a small apartment.

"Kaleen!" Avery called as she closed the door behind us.

"I'm here, but you really should knock, Avery," the girl said, walking in from the hall dressed in the Lukenic uniform.

"Then you should keep the door locked, Kaleen."

Kaleen was just as Avery had described. They looked exactly the same, only Kaleen seemed more sweet, gentle, and kind; her hair was cut short, right above her shoulders.

"Are you twins?" I asked.

"Avery didn't tell you?" Kaleen said with a soft smile.

"She would have figured it out." Avery walked over and fell back onto the couch. Her legs flew up in the air as she dropped. "Kaleen, Mae. Mae, Kaleen."

"It's very nice to meet you, Mae," Kaleen said as she took hold of my hand. "Avery has shared a lot of interesting things about you. It's an honor to have you here."

"Well, there is nothing really interesting about me," I said, laughing nervously.

"Nothing interesting?" Kaleen giggled as she pulled me over to sit on the sofa with her across from Avery. "You don't think your grandfather is interesting?"

"Um, well, most people think he's crazy. Really, all people," I said.

"Still, he's really famous. I mean, from what I heard, he sounds like someone who thinks beyond common logic. You know, sometimes I think you need that. Let's just say I'm a secret fan of his. I've read all his books."

I wasn't sure how to take what Kaleen was saying to me. Meeting someone who didn't know me but was so excited to see me was strange. And the way she talked about Grandpa—I didn't know anyone who talked that way about him. But after everything that had happened, I wasn't ready to trust her interest in him.

"I think his star studies are brave and adventurous."

"Oh, okay," I said.

"I know I'm weird, but I just think it's great to have a different view of things," Kaleen replied. "Can I offer you something to drink?"

"Maybe some water?"

"What about you, Avery?" Kaleen asked as she walked to the kitchen.

"I know where the kitchen is. This used to be my place, too," Avery yelled. She looked at me and whispered,

"I forgot to tell you my sister is nuts."

"Ignore her," Kaleen said, returning with water.

"Thanks," I said, taking the glass from her.

Everything in Kaleen's apartment was so nice. It was hard to imagine a teenager having this space to themselves.

Kaleen sat back down next me. The look in her eye was as if she were about to receive a gift.

"So, your grandfather. I'm so excited to hear from Niles Cefend's own granddaughter about his research."

"Well, he's in jail now because of his *different views*," I replied.

"Yes, I heard."

The room fell silent, and I could see Kaleen's disappointment.

"Kaleen?" Avery started. "He's a madman. That's why he is where he is."

"Yeah, maybe he is mad," Kaleen replied softly. "But aren't you a bit mad yourself, Avery? You carry on like everyone is backward except for you. But isn't that why you are where you are?"

"That's different," Avery protested.

"How?"

"Because what I do doesn't involve things that don't exist, Kaleen. You know, like ghosts and stars."

"Ghosts?" I said, staring at Avery.

"Yeah, ghosts. And I'm the one in the reeducation program. While my sister stays here and talks to ghosts in her free time."

"I'm not the only one who has seen him, Avery. Other students *and* teachers have seen him, too."

"What are you guys talking about? Is there a ghost here?"

"Yes, there is." Kaleen smiled, tilting her head. "But since my sister hasn't seen it, it doesn't exist. But it does. I don't know who he is, but he is very wise."

"You talked to a ghost?" I asked skeptically.

"Yes, I did."

Avery sighed as she shifted her knees up.

"How?" I asked.

"Since the end of the last school year, people have been reporting a man walking around campus and talking to students. The first time I saw him, he was speaking to a group of them. No one had ever seen him before. He talked about things I couldn't really understand."

"Really." I chuckled. "That doesn't sound like a ghost. Aren't ghosts supposed to scare people?"

"He isn't scary. And at first, he doesn't seem like a ghost. He looks real, just as I am standing right here. But whenever you look away, or if a teacher comes, he vanishes."

"Vanishes?" I was starting to understand how people used to see me when I talked about stars. "And you've seen this?"

"Yes, two times. The first with the group of students, and the other time he came to me personally."

"You're crazy," Avery mumbled.

"I can't be crazy if other people have seen him, too," Kaleen snapped. "Anyways, he's like a..." Kaleen paused, thinking of the right words. "I don't know, but he's nothing like I ever experienced.

"Some of the teachers have seen him, but none of them have ever talked with him. He only talks to students. They think he's an intruder who keeps sneaking onto the campus. But it must be a ghost, a ghost of someone who has deep understanding, who just wants to share his wisdom with us."

"So, what did he talk to you about?" I asked.

"Well, he mentioned things about me that most people didn't know. Personal things I never shared with anyone else. And he was talking about Eradeem a lot. He said Eradeem was inadequate and needed freedom. And that there was more to the world than Eradeem."

"See, that doesn't make sense. If he is real, then he's probably a crazy old man," Avery said, sitting up.

"He's actually young and very handsome. That's why, when Avery told me that you tried to leave Eradeem, it made me think of what he said." Kaleen looked deeply into my eyes and took my hand. "Can you tell me about leaving? Like how you even do that?" She scooted closer. "What does that even mean? And your grandfather… Can you tell me what you know about stars, too?"

I slowly pulled back from her, feeling overwhelmed by her interest in me. She wanted to know everything that was going on in my confusing world, but there was nothing I could tell her that wouldn't put me in a deeper hole.

"Whatever you already know is probably all there is to know. The stars are just a made-up story, and I was stupid to be wandering in the woods."

Kaleen blinked a few times, loosening her hold on my hand. I didn't want to disappoint her, but it was the only answer I could give.

Kaleen let me go, walking over to her wide window. She pushed the curtains open, letting the light flood the room and revealing a perfect view of the campus's center. The rare sunlight pierced through the clouds as the sun was setting. She pressed her fingertips against the window and looked up into the sky, focusing on the thick clouds, and then turned off the lights.

"Maybe you think that stars are myths, or a bedtime story parents tell their kids. But I know they are real," Kaleen started. "I was right here when I first saw what I think was a star. I might have been about thirteen. Avery was sleeping, so she didn't see it. I told her, but she didn't believe me. A light fell from the clouds, just like what you might imagine a star would be like.

"I watched it as it came down and landed right in front of the campus statue. I was too afraid to go out to take a look. I'm sure you probably don't believe me either, but I know what I saw was real. Your grandpa isn't crazy. I've seen it myself," Kaleen said. I didn't respond.

Was it Lev's lanterns that she had seen? The same lights that led me deep into the woods? I wondered how many others had seen his lanterns, or even had them in their possession. Just like the old man I'd met on the street.

"I was hoping you might have learned something from your grandpa about stars, and maybe confirmed what I saw."

"I—I don't know," I answered softly. Even though I lied, I wanted to tell her so badly that she wasn't wrong. All I'd ever wanted was someone like Kaleen to talk to. Someone to be excited and wonder about new things with. The reeducation program was making me into someone else, but hearing her story made me feel like my old self for a moment. I'd never thought there was someone else like me. Not being able to talk to someone about everything that had happened when I left Eradeem was hard to bear. But Kaleen was a relief. She didn't know that she was confirming for me that I wasn't imagining things.

"I—I wish I could share more with you, Kaleen," I said, looking away from her. "About Grandpa, and his stars. But I can't."

Kaleen turned to me with a small smile.

"So, you *do* know something?" Kaleen walked back over, then squatted down to my knees like a child waiting to hear a story. I felt my lips twitching to a smile. I couldn't tell if Kaleen understood how serious talking about this type of thing was. But being a product of Lukenic for so long, how she could not? "Please," she said, pulling my hands to her heart. "I won't share what you tell me with anyone."

"N-no, I can't," I responded. The room got quiet again. I could tell

I had both Avery's and Kaleen's attention now.

"Mae's looking for her friend," Avery said, sitting up from the sofa and changing the subject. "She was wondering if you knew her."

"Oh, okay," Kaleen said, sounding disappointed. She let my hand go but continued sitting on the floor. "What's her name?"

"Rita Manna," I replied. "It's her first year here. She would be a ninth grader. Brown, straight hair, taller than me. She just started wearing mask skin on her neck."

"If she came from your old school, then she's an outsider," Avery said.

"Outsider! So, she must be smart, then," said Kaleen.

"Yes, she is," I replied.

"Well, I never heard of her. But it's likely she would be in this building, probably the next floor down. That's where her grade would be."

"Do you think I can take a look to see if she is there?" I asked.

"Of course. No one is stopping you," Kaleen said.

"Well, we have thirty minutes before we have to be back in our room," Avery said as she sat up, taking her feet off the sofa. "So, don't be long. I will be enjoying my freedom here."

Eighteen

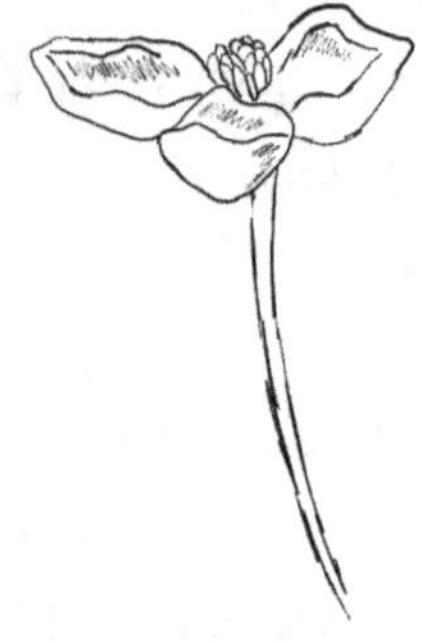

The hallways were less full as I headed down to the second floorSome girls sat talking as others walked in and out of their rooms with their towels for the shower. The hall probably had about twenty doors. I didn't think I could just knock on every single one to find Rita; but if I didn't have any other choice, I would. A girl my age was coming up the stairs into the second-floor hallway. Without hesitating, I stopped her and asked if she knew who Rita was, doing my best to describe her. To my luck, she pointed out Rita's room.

The fifth door on the right side of the hallway. I made my way there, pausing at the door. It had been four months since I last saw her in school. I knew she didn't really want to talk about what had happened out in the woods the night my grandfather was taken away, but I just needed someone who was there that night to help me understand what I'd seen. I raised my fist to knock, then stopped, leaving my fist in the air. I remembered her mother and the things she'd said to me that last time I was at their house. I wasn't supposed to come around Rita anymore.

Even though we were not at Rita's house and her mother wouldn't know, I was beginning to wonder if Rita was feeling the same as her mother about me. Maybe that was the reason Rita never reached out to me. She'd never tried to come over again after she'd picked up her camera; she'd never even called me. Even if my parents told me that I couldn't see my best friend anymore, I would still try. Now that I was here and able to see her, I wasn't so sure I wanted to. As I turned away from Rita's door, it opened.

"Mae?" said a voice from behind me. I turned around to find Rita standing at the door. Her jaw dropped as she looked me up and down, seeing me in a Lukenic uniform.

I gave a nervous laugh as I dropped my hands behind me.

"Hey, Rita." I felt so out of place. "Surprise!"

Rita wasn't in uniform. She was wearing a loose shirt and shorts, her usual sleep and study wear.

"What are you doing here?" she asked. Her tone was irritated, as I'd feared. I'd hoped she would be happily shocked to see me, ending with hugs and laughter, followed by a friendly *What are you doing here!?* But her voice only confirmed that I didn't belong.

"Well, I came to see you. It's been a really long time for friends to not see each other," I said.

"Oh, okay," Rita replied, shifting her weight from side to side. "Well, I'm surprised to see you here, in Lukenic, in a Lukenic uniform."

"Yeah." I chuckled. "Can we go somewhere to talk? I can explain everything."

"I don't know. I really need to get to my studies, Mae." I almost didn't know what to say. I didn't even think there was another option other than talking to your best friend who you had been separated from. I knew she valued her studies, but I couldn't even fathom why she would consider her studies over me at this time.

"Okay," I said.

"So, this is how you're going to treat me now. Your mom told me you can't talk to me anymore. Is that what you really mean by you have to go study?"

"No!" Rita said, leaving silence between us. What happened that things had changed so much? Rita took a deep breath as she looked down the hall. "Okay. Can we go outside? We can talk there."

I followed her outside to the front of the dorm building under a large tree.

"Okay," Rita said with her arms folded to her chest. "What's going on?"

I could hardly even look at her. This wasn't my friend anymore. It was like I was barely anyone to her now, and she was doing me a favor. I kept my hands at my sides, pulling the end of my skirt, trying not to get emotional.

"Sorry if me being here disturbs you. But I thought we were friends."

She took a deep breath with no words to follow. So, I continued.

"They sent me here to Lukenic for a program on the other side of campus that's off-limits to the students here. It's for troubled students. So, don't worry, I won't be anywhere near you. I got sent here because I got caught near the border."

"What were you doing there?" Rita asked.

"I don't know. I was feeling lonely. I didn't have anyone to talk to. I thought maybe I could keep going until I ran into Lev again."

"Lev?" Rita asked.

"Yeah, it's the name of the person I met that night I was lost."

"That's really stupid, Mae. We should have never gone as far as we did in the first place. And then you go off looking for some stranger, who I am guessing you haven't told anyone about."

"Okay, well, you weren't there for me," I said.

"So, it's my fault."

"I'm not saying that."

"Okay, then what are you saying?"

This wasn't going anywhere. Rita was the only person who understood me. But things were changing.

"Maybe this was a mistake. Maybe I should have just stayed where I was."

"Look, okay. Yes, my mother doesn't want me to hang around you anymore, not since she learned I got accepted here and that I almost lost my opportunity because of that night. She was furious with me, Mae. Things aren't that easy for me."

"Then why do you have a problem with me, if it's your mom!" I shouted. "You think it's been easy for me? My grandpa's in jail, and they put me in a program I don't want to be in. To reeducate me from any teaching Grandpa ever taught me. My parents didn't even tell me. They just sent me away! I thought I would at least have you." Tears built up in my eyes, but Rita only looked away from me.

"Is there anything else, Mae?" she replied. "Is this why you came here?"

"No, it's not. I wanted to tell you that I'm not crazy, that I did meet someone out in the woods, and I have proof that what I saw was real. I don't have it with me, but if you check your camera…"

"Mae, what are you talking about?"

"I took a picture of him, and you can see that the woods look different. It's proof I wasn't in Eradeem."

"What?"

"Somehow I wasn't in Eradeem. I was outside past the desert. That's why no one could find me. It may sound crazy; I mean, I thought I was going crazy until I saw the picture I took. If you have your camera with you, you can just go look."

Rita took a deep breath, folding her arms to her chest.

"Let me guess, you saw stars, too."

I started to speak but stopped. I was so desperate to see her I didn't think about how this would all sound. It had built inside of me, and she was the only person I felt safe telling, but she was looking at me like everyone else used to do when I first started school.

"If you could just go through your camera back to the time I disappeared, there is a man in it. It will have a time stamp. It proves I'm not lying."

"Mae, I honestly don't have time for this. I tried helping you, and I seriously saw a change in you. But your grandfather being taking away has brought this part of you back that I just can't help."

"So, this whole time you were only my friend because you felt sorry for me."

"No."

"Okay, then it was that you could get help from my family to get into Lukenic."

"I was your friend before I knew all of that, as I already told you!"

"Everyone knew who my grandfather was, so don't play dumb."

"That's not true!" Rita shouted. I really wanted to believe her, but the person standing in front of me was someone else entirely.

"Okay," Rita said, taking in another deep breath. "So now what?" she said, adjusting her folded arms.

"I don't know."

"Well, I think we should forget about everything and just move on."

Rita had nothing to say. It seemed like our friendship was officially over.

Nineteen

I felt more alone than ever after talking to Rita. All I wanted was to go back to how things used to be, when it was just me and Grandpa. But I couldn't expect that my grandfather would always be there to protect me from the world. He could at least have prepared me for how people would perceive me. Then Rita wouldn't have pretended to be kind to me.

I looked around the classroom as my four classmates sat watching the same video we had watched the month before. I wondered how bad things were for them that their parents had no choice but to send them to this place.

None of them gave details about why they'd been sent here. A room of kids who weren't good enough, who needed to be changed. We were all so different in personality; the only thing that tied us together was this program.

That day I was given a progress report from Mr. Owns. It said I was doing well in the program but I wasn't considered rehabilitated yet. I wasn't sure what else needed to happen before I'd be able to leave. As usual, once class was over, Avery was gone; but now I knew where she was. I made it outside of the dorm to the courtyard, searching for Theo and Dime, but they weren't at our usual spot. I figured instead of waiting around for them that maybe I just needed to be alone.

I ventured to the middle of campus, where I hadn't yet explored. There, in the courtyard, was a beautiful statue of a woman reading a book. It was as desolate as the rest of the campus, but still lovely. The bottom was covered with moss that crept up to her tunic. I moved to view the rest of her when I was startled by the presence of another person. A man stood on the other side of the statue. His eyes met mine, but my instinct to leave failed me. I blinked as I found it difficult to look away from him. Something in his eyes felt familiar.

"Hello." He smiled, raising his hand to wave.

"Hi," I responded sheepishly. He was young and handsome. His black hair hung above his eyes. He had his hands tucked into his dark jacket. I thought maybe he was lost.

"Are you a student here?" the man asked, walking around towards the front of the statue, studying it closely.

"Yes, I am." I took hold of my arm, not sure what to do. We were told not to talk to anyone from the other side of campus.

"Then maybe *you* can tell me," he said, seeming to be talking about the statue.

I hesitated, approaching slowly, still trying to understand where I knew him from. I moved closer and my skin went cold.

"D-do we know each other?" I asked.

He looked at me, and I found myself frozen, searching his eyes. "We do."

My heart raced as my mouth fell open. I wanted to say it, but I couldn't. The man took a step towards me, placing his hand on my head. I closed my eyes as the words slipped through my lips.

"Lev." I felt a quiver in my chest as my eyes opened.

His face brightened just as it had when he'd found his lost baby sheep in the woods.

"Hello, Mae."

I wasn't sure how I knew it was Lev. It had been dark when I'd first met him, but seeing him in daylight was like seeing him for the first time. I could see the bronze glow of his complexion and the dark vastness of his eyes. The same gentleness seemed to surround me just like before.

"I'm trying to figure out what this girl is reading," Lev said, folding his hands behind his back as he turned to the statue. I tried to focus on what Lev was saying, but my mind was still trying to accept that he was right here beside me at Lukenic.

"I—I don't know," I stammered.

"Actually, the answer is nothing. She isn't reading anything because she is just a statue," he replied with a satisfied smirk.

"Oh, okay," I said, slightly confused. "Am I dreaming right now?"

"Well, you weren't dreaming before."

I tried to process that, but I didn't really know what to think.

"It's really good to see you again, Mae."

"I thought you weren't real."

Lev chuckled, turning back to me.

"You've been wondering if everything that happened that night was real, and it's my fault you feel that way but that night *was* real, Mae."

"So, then, I was really outside of Eradeem?"

"Yes, you were."

"How? How did I leave Eradeem without passing the border and crossing over the desert? How is it possible that I was missing for hours, and then suddenly I was in my bedroom?"

He glanced away, staring into the distance. "Do you remember the story I told you?"

I didn't expect him to bring that up. I paused, trying to remember. "You mean about a king who died trying to save his girlfriend? Her name was—"

"Premleen," he said, turning back. "There was something I didn't tell you."

I was quiet, wondering where he was going with this.

Lev walked around the statue, observing it more as he spoke. "I didn't tell you that the king isn't actually dead. Yes, he died. But he didn't stay that way."

"Okay," I said with a timid smile.

"After the king lost his life for his beloved, the counselor rescued the king one last time. The counselor saved the king by becoming one with him, and all the power the counselor possessed now belonged to the king."

"Power? What power?"

"Supernatural power. Remember I told you that when Premleen brought the curse to Light, everyone was affected; but the counselor was the one who rescued the king, taking him to safety. When the counselor gave up his life, merging with the king, the king was able to do what he did for Premleen for the entire City of Light. Wipe away the curse without losing his new life."

"You mean the Abnormal?"

Lev turned, facing me from the other side of the statue. "Exactly. Unfortunately, with this new power came a new obstacle. Unless the people knew him, there was nothing the king could do for them."

I glanced away, trying to remember the story. "But you said that everyone in Light knew the king, almost personally."

"Yes, but since they believed the king was dead, something strange happened. The king had no way into the city. An invisible barrier stood between him and Light."

"Why?"

"The curse activated a barrier against the king now that he was no longer human. Premleen herself even went into the city to tell the people the truth, but they rejected her. They accused her of killing the king, and she was banished from the city. The only way the king would have access to the city was if just one person with the curse's mark knew he still existed."

I wrapped my arms across my shoulders. I didn't know why Lev's story intrigued me so much. It sounded like a fairy tale. Maybe I was interested because of how often Grandpa would talk about the Abnormal.

"When I was younger, people would say that the Abnormal was going to happen to everyone. I'm afraid of the Abnormal happening to me. I'm afraid of what it's doing to my mother. She's..."

"Mae." I looked up as Lev approached me. His eyes where serious, and I could see some anger there, too. "The old king is the answer. For the first time in a long time, he finally has the access he needs to this city. He lives, Mae, and he's come back."

"I don't understand."

"Yes." Lev chuckled. "This is why the lanterns were sent out to Eradeem, to share the truth with anyone who might believe. Even though the message is discreet, a little truth is better than nothing. A little truth can open wonder. Wonder leads to questions, and questions lead the mind to find what's true. The truth of what really lies beyond the border. But meeting you, Mae, has changed everything."

I tilted my head, as I could only glare at him. I couldn't understand how anything he was saying related to me.

"You don't believe me?"

"I'm not sure what to believe. I don't even know if this is really happening."

"Mae." Lev took my hands in his. I looked down, feeling the warmth and the texture of his flesh. His hands engulfed mine, and I could feel the callouses on his palms. Everything about him felt so real. His eyes narrowed, like he might cry; but he didn't.

"Who told you that your eyes are not to be trusted? I stand before you, and you seem like you don't trust me, but I know you do. Even though you barely know me, there is something in your heart that has allowed what I have said to take residence inside you. You are very special, Mae. It might be the childlikeness you carry, or how you were brought up in life. But I am extremely grateful. You have no idea."

The warmth of my tears dared to spill, but I couldn't understand why. I couldn't explain it, but I felt it in how Lev's hands held mine.

"So, what do I have to do with any of this? I've never met any king."

Lev let go of my hands and only smiled. "You wanted to know how you could cross the desert, how you left Eradeem?"

"Yeah, you never answered my question."

"A rip in the barrier."

"A rip in the barrier? What does that mean?"

Lev dropped his hands to his sides as he stared at the ground.

"You only know about the wall that traps Eradeem from the outside world, but beyond that wall, the place I first met you, is an invisible barrier. No one can go through it. The king became so frustrated with the curse, he used his power to destroy the barrier. For days and days, he tried to break it, not sure what it would accomplish.

The situation was causing him to lose hope for Eradeem. It almost destroyed him—until one day, something happened. The king made a rip in the barrier. He could see Eradeem from the other side, but he couldn't go through it. Animals from the outside could go through it, even people, but not him. It looked like he still wouldn't have access to Eradeem. Then he realized that anyone in Eradeem could have access to him. He hoped that the lanterns would trigger someone's curiosity who would one day find that rip in the barrier and find their way outside."

"Wait, I was under the impression that this happened a long time ago."

"That's correct."

I opened my mouth to speak, but nothing came out. I took a dry swallow, feeling my heart threatening to burst from my chest.

"Everyone thinks I'm nuts, that's why I'm here in the school to be fixed. I just want to go home. I want things to go back to normal," I cried.

"I want the same thing. I want things to go back to normal. Mae, you have done enough, and I know you are already suffering. Because of you, I'm here right now. I have my feet planted on this ground, in this land; and for that, I am extremely grateful. I can't make you do or believe in something you don't want to; but I know your heart cannot resist the truth, no matter how uncomfortable it makes you. It's just not in you."

Lev took a deep breath and smiled. "This is just the beginning. Change is coming, and I will make sure there will be no more Abnormal. The more people who know the truth, the easier it will be to make right what has been done wrong."

"Why are you telling me this?"

"Because whether you share the truth of Eradeem or keep it to yourself and enjoy a normal life…. whatever you decide, I will be with you." Lev looked behind me, and I followed his gaze to the tree branch. The cardinal was there, sitting on the branch like a pop of color in this ugly world I was living in.

"It's that bird again," I said, looking back at Lev, but no one was there. I spun around the other way, and still, I saw no one. "Lev," I called, but the only one there was the bird and me.

Twenty

I was starting to wonder if I was hallucinating like Ms. Vivly said I had been. Why was I suddenly seeing Lev out of nowhere? How could I trust myself? Fane thought I was good, normal, someone to emulate. But I was beginning to think that maybe I needed the reeducation more than anyone. After seeing Lev, the next day I stayed in my room during free time. I figured if I wasn't interacting with the other problem students, it might help. Plus, I wondered if maybe I was a danger to everyone around me.

Surprisingly, though, Avery came looking for me. I was lying on my side with my pillow hugged to my chest as she entered our room. I was shocked she wasn't already off to her usual spot on the other side. She leaned against the doorframe, looking at me.

"So, I forgot to tell you last night, my sister wants to see you again."

"What for?" I asked, pushing my pillow up to my face. I'd really thought my room would be a good place to keep out of trouble.

"She probably wants to pick your brain on some stuff about stars or whatever. She wanted me to make sure you'll be over there tonight."

"I don't know," I said, rolling over to face the wall. "I just want to sleep till tomorrow. I'm trying my best to stay out of trouble." I pulled the covers over my head, tucking my knees to my chest. "I think I really do need this program, Avery."

"Are you crazy?" she said, as she yanked the blanket from me. "You don't need this stupid program; don't let them brainwash you, Mae. There is nothing wrong with you. You're a cool person, you know that? I would hate you if you were normal."

I turned back over, seeing Avery hovering over me with her hands on her hips.

"But you don't understand," I started, but she put her palm in the air to silence me.

"Look, just come over when you're ready, okay? Make sure no one sees you and do what we did last time. I'm sure you can find Kaleen's apartment; just don't go directly after me. I'll see you there." She gave me one final glare before leaving the room, closing the door behind her.

I sat up on my bed, staring at the closed door. I wished I could just not care, but it was hard not being influenced by Avery. She was refreshing to be around, no matter what Fane said about her. She had a way of making you do what she wanted with her devil-may-care attitude. Her short speech broke my bad mood, and soon after she left, I was out the door to the other side of campus. I wandered around before going through the broken fence, and once I was on the other side, I checked that no one was watching before coming out.

I didn't rush over to Kaleen's dorm like we did before. I took my time, taking in the real Lukenic. Everyone here was so beautiful. It was much nicer than my school back home. There were more trees here, and although the buildings where old, they didn't look it. This was the school that my parents and grandparents had attended. If my life were normal, I would be here, too. All the kids who went here got a leg up in society; but, so far, I wasn't heading in the right direction because of Grandpa, because of the chemicals.

I was getting tired of being an outsider, being the one who thought different, being the one who didn't get it. I had only changed who I was on the outside the year before because I was afraid of what would happen to Grandpa. I didn't allow my thoughts to change, because I just didn't want to let go of myself. Looking around the large campus, the beautiful students, and the expensive old buildings made me regret the time I'd lost. If I had listened to my teachers and done what I was told the first time, I wouldn't be where I was. Maybe I could have been one of these students.

Once I was in the dorm, I went directly to Kaleen's room. Avery poked her head out from the door.

"Mae!" she said, seeming a bit surprised. "So!" she started as she peeked behind her. "I guess Kaleen isn't the only one who wants to meet you."

"What do you mean not the only one?" I could hear other voices in the room. Avery leaned out to look down the hall before pulling me inside. She quickly closed the door, locking it. I walked into the midst of a group of students scattered throughout Avery's apartment. When they noticed me, everyone got quiet. Their eyes were all on me.

"I swear I had no idea all these people would be here," Avery said as she emerged from the group.

"I'm sorry, Mae," Kaleen said. "I only told a few of my friends about you, but it looks like our whole club found out. I promise that no one outside of this room will know about you being here."

"A club? What club?"

"Well, this is our Niles Cefend Fan Base and Strange Phenomenon Club," Kaleen said, stepping aside to present about twelve other students. "It's a secret club where we come together and discuss Niles Cefend studies and other strange phenomenon. We added the 'strange phenomenon' part once the ghost started showing up at our school last year. We're very exclusive; you don't have to worry about anyone finding out."

"See, I told you she was weird," Avery whispered.

"Everyone, this is Mae Meadows, granddaughter of our beloved Niles Cefend." The students clapped softly, some even standing like I was a guest speaker. They looked at me as if I were carrying some profound wisdom.

"Mae was extremely close to her grandfather and knows all the things he was working on before he was taken away."

"Wait!" I stopped Kaleen, pulling her to the side. "How did you know that about me and my grandfather?"

"Oh! Your friend Rita told me. She said you guys were best friends. I saw you talking to her that night you were here, but don't worry. I didn't tell her about this meeting."

"Okay, but..." I started as my mind went blank. My jaw was left hanging while Kaleen stared at me. How was I supposed to explain to her that I no longer believed in my grandfather? The struggle for my sanity just wouldn't end. A community of people suddenly came into existence, and somehow, I had to talk about my crazy grandfather, who they all dearly admired as if I still held their beliefs.

"What am I supposed to do exactly?" I asked, forcing a smile. "I wasn't expecting this at all." I was a bit rebellious, sure, but I was a people pleaser, too. Seeing how excited Kaleen was to have me here, it was hard to refuse her request.

"I guess just tell them a little about yourself and your relationship with your grandpa. And maybe something about what he was last researching. I hope you aren't mad, Mae, but it's truly an honor for my club to have you here."

"I'm not upset, just surprised," I said, scanning the room of students.

"You don't need to be nervous. We all love your grandpa here."

"But…" I started, but Kaleen walked away to address her club.

"Mae is a bit nervous; she wasn't expecting all of us. As you know, Avery, my twin sister, is on the other side of campus for reeducation. Most of the school doesn't know anything about that program or that there are other students there. Because of how our society feels about Niles Cefend, they put him in a prison to protect us from his brilliant mind, and now they have sent his granddaughter to the reeducation program to rid her of any knowledge Niles Cefend bestowed upon her." The students conversed among themselves and seemed excited. "We just hope that she still has a little of Niles Cefend in her to share with us," Kaleen finished.

My mouth dried as I tried to swallow. For four years I was told that my grandfather was poisoning me, and for three of those years I did my best to ignore it. Regardless of what anyone had to say about Grandpa, there was freedom in stretching my mind to wonder about the unknown, whether proven or not. Whether nonsense or practical, whether true or false. But now I was in front of people who wanted to hear what I had to say, as I was coming to terms with the fact that maybe Grandpa was wrong about everything.

Your heart cannot resist the truth, no matter how uncomfortable it makes you. It's not you.

Lev's voice echoed in my mind, like a ghost reminding me of my past. But was that really his voice I'd heard yesterday? Was there even a man called Lev? My eyes squeezed shut as I covered my face with my palms. Why was it so hard to just let everything go? Why couldn't I just accept what I was being told? I took in a deep breath as I searched for myself, trying to tap back into who I used to be. Was she even still there? Was she too weak to speak? I had decided earlier today to officially kill her off for the sake of being normal. But now I was being asked to free her from her cage.

"Are you okay...?" Kaleen asked, still standing beside me.

"Yeah," I replied, thinking of how to start. "I've..." I said, looking around the room, then to Avery. "I've been hiding a lot of things to keep my family and myself safe." My hands trembled as the small crowd of students leaned in to listen. I was surprised: who I used to be had spoken up without hesitation; she was confident in what she knew. I hated her, but I also found that I missed her too much to let this moment slip away.

"I was raised by my grandfather. Most of my education came from him. He hid the fact that I wasn't attending normal school from my parents, who worked away from home for years. It wasn't until four years ago, in the fifth grade, that I started real school. I had no idea that the things Grandpa taught me were forbidden and seen as ludicrous. I talked a lot about his studies, but I learned from my teachers that my grandfather was no longer considered a brilliant man. For a while I didn't care what they said about him.

"I was told to stop sharing my grandfather's crazy studies with the other students, but I didn't, even though I was humiliated by my teachers because of it. Then they threatened to remove Grandpa from our home if I didn't stop spreading his ideas, and so I finally did. But the next year he was taken anyway. I don't know exactly what Grandpa's last research was on, but I know that whatever it was must be why they took him away."

Everyone in he room zeroed in on me, not wanting to miss a word. I took another deep breath before continuing.

"I think Grandpa somehow contacted the outside world. Somewhere beyond the border, and beyond the desert." I looked down, breaking my eye contact with the room full of students.

Chatter filled the air. I could see Kaleen and Avery had not been expecting to hear me say anything like that.

"I know this, because I've been to the outside." I glanced up as they tried whispering among themselves. Avery and Kaleen just stared at me. Avery's eyes narrowed at me, but Kaleen's were wide as she smiled. I looked at Kaleen and saw the familiar wonder I'd once had. "It—it was the ghost who took me there." The room erupted with indistinguishable chatter.

"Quiet, everyone," Kaleen said, trying to calm everyone down. "What do you mean, the ghost took you?" She shushed the room.

"When you told me about the ghost last time, I didn't know who you meant. But then yesterday he came to me, the same person who took me over the border. He told me he wanted people to know the truth. Eradeem's true history."

I stopped myself before continuing, thinking about Lev. I had battled over the truth of his existence; yet the fact was, whether he was a hallucination or a ghost, he had captivated me in a way I couldn't deny. All I'd wanted to do that day was sleep and forget about what had happened the day before. But there was something inside me that wouldn't let go of Lev. I was already seen as crazy; what more did I have to lose?

"The ghost... His name is Lev."

"Lev," Kaleen repeated.

"I think he may be a ghost of a king." I watched as the room talked amonged themselves. I couldn't tell what they were thinking of me, but I let that go. Kaleen took my hand, leading me to a spot in the room where I could sit down in front of everyone.

"Tell us," Kaleen said, finding a chair to sit. "Tell us his story."

Twenty One

I told the students everything Lev had told me. I wasn't one hundred percent sure if I trusted what I was telling them, but it felt so good to do it. Afterward, Avery told me she had officially put me on her list of crazy people; but she didn't treat me any differently. She did tell Theo and Dime about me leaving Eradeem, which I didn't appreciate, but they obviously didn't believe her. Who would believe a story like that other than the Niles Cefend Fan Base and Strange Phenomenon Club?

Over the next few weeks, I continued to meet with the club. Avery and I had decided we would take turns going to the other side, so no one got suspicious about why we were both suddenly nowhere to be found, and one could vouch for the other if anyone asked. I brought them the book my grandfather was last studying, including his notes. The club was shocked that it was a children's book, but it intrigued them even more. The fact that the story Lev had told me seemed to parallel the book Grandpa was studying got the club overly excited.

After a few weeks of this, I finally heard back from Marty. He was able to make plans to take me to see Grandpa. I didn't tell the club I was meeting with Grandpa; I wanted to keep it to myself. He got permission from Ms. Lowkuss, saying that I had a doctor's appointment and that my parents had approved it.

Because Marty was in the military, the school didn't question him. Still, I was nervous all day waiting for the time when he would come and get me. Mr. Owns's last class couldn't end fast enough. When it finally did, I quickly but calmly gathered my things and headed to my room to change my clothes. I rushed up the stairs, but I was suddenly stopped. Fane called out to me as he tried to catch up.

"Mae!" he said, running up the stairs behind me. "Where are you going? Are you in a rush or something?" he asked. "You left the class pretty fast."

"Oh, I didn't mean to," I said. "But I do have somewhere to go."

"Well, do you have a minute?"

"Sure?"

Fane walked up the staircase toward me, leaving two steps between us, making our heights the same. It was nice to look him directly in his eyes.

"Well," Fane started as he clutched his books to his side, his other hand on the rail. He put one foot on the next step and leaned closer to me. "You may think this is weird, but I've just been concerned about you."

"Really?" I said, my body stiffening as I held my books closer to my chest. It was weird for him to say something like that to me, since we didn't really know one another. Since that day in the abandoned track, we hadn't really talked much. But a guy like him even considering my well-being was guaranteed to make me timid, and a little proud at the same time. Avery walked up the stairs past us, giving me her usual confused stare. Fane turned to look at her, but she acted as if she didn't notice us. Once she had passed, Fane continued.

"For instance, your friend Avery? You guys are nothing alike. And I honestly think she can learn a lot from you."

"You think so?" I said, shifting my weight to one side. Avery was like three years older than me. What could she possibly learn from me?

"Yes," Fane said. "You're a good student, Mae. You do what you are told. You follow the rules. You really seem like you're doing well in this program. But Avery, she's not. She breaks the rules and sometimes goes outside with her mask off. She has no respect. She isn't a good influence."

"She's the only other girl here, and we are roommates, so it would be hard not to be friends."

"I understand, but you shouldn't look up to her." He leaned towards me as he tried not to be loud. "If she continues like this, she isn't going to amount to much, and I definitely don't want to see you like that. You're a good girl and, honestly, I think you don't really need to be in this program, not like the rest of these screw-ups."

I didn't know how I could be considered special. I only tried to be on my best behavior so I could leave this place as soon as possible.

"Okay, well, I do have to go, Fane."

"All right." He sighed. "Just stay out of trouble, okay?" Fane went back down the stairs.

As I walked away from him, I began to wonder: What did he mean? Did he know about us going over to the other side of Lukenic, or was he just saying all of that randomly? But I didn't really have time to think on it.

I headed straight to my room, dropping my books onto my bed.

"What was that all about?" Avery said, lying down in her bed.

"What do you mean?" I quickly took off my uniform, looking for something to wear.

"You and Fane. Does he have a thing for you or something?"

"Um, I don't know," I said.

"Well, I hope not. He's kind of weird. Most boys like him would be all over me, but he's not."

"I don't know. He seems like the kind of guy who likes following the rules."

"Really?" Avery sat up. "If he's such a goody-goody, why is he here?"

"I don't know. He never told me why he was in this program, but I gotta go."

"Where are you going?"

"Doctor's appointment." I walked out of the room.

Marty came early to pick me up. We drove for about an hour before we finally reached the facility. We went past the front gate of the prison and then around to a maintenance garage on the other side. A couple of officer cars sat nearby, and gardening equipment lay scattered around the area. Marty pulled the car up to the side of the building and parked. "Just wait here until I wave for you to come over, okay?"

"How long is it going to take?"

"Hopefully not long."

As Marty began to leave the car, he paused and turned back to me. "There is something I need to tell you after we're done here."

"Is there something wrong?" But Marty didn't reply. He looked away and left me in the car. I shrank down in my seat as my nerves got stirred up.

"What was that about?" I whispered to myself. I watched Marty walk into the garage and through a door. Then it really hit me. What the heck was I doing here? I was starting to feel like this was too much for me. This was what I wanted, right?

About ten minutes later, Marty signaled for me to come in. I followed his orders, leaving the car and walking to him as if I were trying to not be seen. He closed the door behind me. Inside the hallway, half the lights were turned off. Marty walked ahead of me. He looked back to be sure we weren't being followed. He kept quiet as we traveled down the halls, and I did my best to do the same. I did hear some voices, but I didn't really know where they were coming from. Since Marty didn't pay much mind to them, I ignored them as well. Once we were at the end of the hallway, we turned left. In the next hallway, the lights were bright until we made a right into a very dark one with a door at the end. The door had a small window, and I could see a dim light coming from it.

"Almost there," Marty said. Once we came to the door, Marty took out a single key to unlock it. There was another man standing in the room. He took a quick glance at me, then nodded for Marty to follow him. He led us to a room with a metal door. The other man stopped and turned to me, patting me down to check for anything that could be used to help Grandpa escape. Once done, he opened the door wide for me to go in. The door led to a dark room with one small window bringing in the outside light. "Go ahead, we'll be out here waiting for you. You have ten minutes," Marty said. Things were happening so fast; I felt like I needed more time to prepare.

"What are you waiting for?" the man holding the door said. "Go in." The door's shadow eclipsed his face, blocking out his eyes. I started to walk, taking small steps, realizing that I couldn't turn back now.

Once I was fully in the room, the door closed behind me. I scanned the space and saw nothing. No chair or table. Just an empty room. But in the darkest corner, I could tell something was there. It seemed to move slightly.

"Mae?" It was the crackly, dry voice of an old man.

I took a step toward the voice.

"Grandpa," I said softly, hesitant. "Is that you?"

The dark corner soon became a figure, and then an old man stepped out. A smaller, older version of my grandfather was before me. His hair and beard were whiter and longer than before. He was wearing a gray prison uniform that hung from his body.

"Mae, what are you doing here? How did you get here?" he asked as his voice became clearer and more familiar.

"Grandpa!" I said, breaking down into tears and running into his weak arms. He held me with what little strength he had, then fell to his knees, crying.

"I miss you so much," I said, laying over his shoulder and kissing his head.

He pulled away from me to get a better look. "Is everything okay?"

In those first moments of seeing Grandpa again, I desperately wished that everything that had happened after he was taken away could just slip from my mind. But the look in his eyes reminded me of the world I lived in; I could only imagine what he was going through.

"I'm fine," I said, taking hold of him again. My tears soaked into his clothes, and I wished we were both home.

"What about your mother and father?" he whispered in my ear. "Are they okay? I just don't understand why you're here."

"Grandpa, I have to tell you something," I said, turning my face to speak into his ear. "I saw them," I said quietly.

"Saw what?" Grandpa said. I pulled away from him so I could see his face.

"I saw the stars. I was on the outside, and I saw them with my own eyes. You were contacted by someone from the outside, weren't you? That's why you're here, isn't it?" I wasn't sure what to expect next, but he became silent, and I felt the mood change. Grandpa's eyes narrowed as his jaw stiffened.

"How did you get here?" Grandpa asked, slurring his words.

"Marty, he brought me."

"Marty?" Grandpa tilted his head down, glaring at me.

"Yes," I replied. But I suddenly felt that I had done something wrong. "I was so worried about you the day they took you."

"No," Grandpa said suddenly. "Don't talk about that. I was wrong, Mae. I shouldn't have filled your mind with stars. I'm so sorry for what I have done. Forgive me." Grandpa fell to the floor at my feet with his face down. "Why would they do this to me?" he cried from the ground. I bent to touch his shoulder, but he flinched. "How could they use you against me like this?"

"What?" I said, feeling confused. "Grandpa, you don't understand. You were right about the stars. No one is using me."

"You shouldn't be here, Mae. You must grow up and be a normal adult. Not like me. You need to live."

"But Grandpa, you aren't listening," I protested.

"I heard you, Mae, and you need to stay away from me." He stood, walking to the door. "I'm a sick man." Grandpa banged on the door. "We are done here. She can go. Take me back to my cell."

"Grandpa," I said, standing where he had left me. I didn't know what had happened. I didn't know if I'd said something wrong. He held on to the doorknob, turning it over and over again as if he were afraid of me. He never looked back at me, only demanded to leave the room. The door opened as a man came in, placing handcuffs on Grandpa's wrists. The guard checked Grandpa for anything I might have given him and then he walked Grandpa out.

I stood there in the same place. I watched the door, not even noticing Marty coming to get me. He said something, but I didn't hear him. I only felt him taking me by the arm and leading me out of the room. It wasn't until we were outside in the crisp cold that I was aware of anything again.

"So, what did he say? You didn't stay with him very long," Marty asked once we were in the car.

I was still trying to understand what had happened. Grandpa was happy to see me. Our family reunion had been filled with joy, but it'd ended with disappointment, from both Grandpa and me.

"I… I don't know," I replied. "I was just trying to figure out what went wrong, or if something happened to him. He said he wanted me to be normal. What did they do to him?"

"Did you say anything that might have set him off?" Marty asked.

"I–I'm not sure."

Marty started the car, and we headed back to Lukenic.

"They did something to him," I said, staring at the ground.

"It's not your fault, just a misunderstanding," Marty said. I turned to look at him. What could he possibly mean by that?

"What are you talking about?"

"Well, there was something I needed to tell you. But I thought it would be best until after you saw Grandpa."

"What is it?" I asked. Marty kept his eyes on the road. He did not even glance over to me.

"There is a reason for the wall, Mae. It's to protect us."

"From what?"

"There are dangerous chemicals that linger over the border, and they can cause hallucinations."

"But I was told it's not so dangerous anymore; only a small percentage get really affected from the border."

"Well, they found a dangerous amount in Grandpa's system. At some point, Grandpa may have gotten too close. I'm sure the chemicals started his obsession with his stars."

I didn't respond right away. I was trying to process what he was saying, but I only felt more confused.

"So, you are saying that he was hallucinating?"

"I'm sorry. But it's true. I'm sure Grandpa knows this now. But he obviously never believed that it was chemicals near the house that were making him crazy. Since I work in the military, they made sure that we wouldn't be affected. Our medical injections prevent us from getting sick." I didn't respond; I had heard all of this before already. So, he continued. "I held off from telling you. I wanted you to see for yourself."

I was so tired of trying to believe in something. I had given in to hope, and it was just proving how wrong I was. I really couldn't say anything else. So, I didn't. I just let the scenery sink in. As I rested my head against the window, I watched as everything passed by, and a dim reflection looked back at me. I didn't recognize her anymore. I was not at all who I'd thought I was.

Twenty Two

Everyone could tell something was different when I returned from the prison. I didn't talk for days. Not a single word. It was as if my mind was ripped apart. The only thing I could do was sleep to turn off my thoughts, hoping that my dreams wouldn't continue to torture me. I felt untrustworthy, tainted. Seeing my grandpa in that state played in my mind every day. When class ended, I stayed shut away in my room, lying in bed. If I couldn't sleep, I would stare at the wall, trying to forget Grandpa's skeletal face. But I did remember, and I broke down crying. It physically hurt thinking about him.

I began to resent Grandpa. Hatred grew in my heart for him; and at the same time, I felt so sad for him. Grandpa's obsession had become more important than his granddaughter growing up normal and healthy. It felt safe to say he was sick, after everything he had been through. I regretted that that was the moment he'd felt like telling me to turn away from everything he'd taught me.

I was finally accepting that it was best I be at Lukenic, and that maybe the school could reverse the damage already done to me. I was slowly taking in the teachings. What everyone had said about stars, I was starting to believe.

I stopped going to meet with my grandfather's fan club. I always made up an excuse. Avery watched me in my depressed state, trying to get out of me what was wrong, but I shut her out. I didn't understand why it mattered to her. She didn't believe the stories I told her anyway.

One day, I looked in the mirror before class and saw my Abnormal. A vine-like red mark on the right side of my collarbone peeking up my neck. The mark over my heart was no longer a small leaf. It had spread across a quarter of my chest. My rite of passage was finally here. I rubbed my neck, feeling the texture of the Abnormal on my skin. It stung a bit, but not enough to feel painful. I had dreaded the day that this would happen, but it wasn't so bad, I thought. I found a mask piece my mother had packed for me and applied it, blending it into my skin with makeup. I could feel a small burning sensation where the mark was, which I knew was normal with a new mark.

I slept every day during break. It didn't take long before Avery just got over it and started ignoring me. Theo tried to get me to talk. When that didn't work, he tried to get me to leave my room. Sometimes, I noticed Dime looking over at me. He hardly ever looked at anyone.

Fane didn't say a word to me. He went on as normal until, suddenly one day, he approached me. I'd decided to come out of my room into the lounge on the first floor. I leaned against the sofa arm with my knees pulled up to my chest, staring out the window. Fane saw me from outside, then made his way in, smiling as he walked over to a seat near me. I kept my gaze out the window. It was obvious that he wanted to talk. He sat there for a moment, hunched over, as he rested his arms on his legs. Yes, I was out of my room finally, but I had no intention of interacting with anyone.

"So, how much longer do you have here?" Fane asked, but I ignored him. I figured the less I talked, the faster he would go away. "You've been here awhile. You should know by now. Rumor has it that you're here because of your grandfather." He waited for me to respond, but still, I said nothing.

He let out a heavy sigh and leaned back against the sofa. "What's so interesting outside that's got your attention?" he asked, following my gaze out the window.

Something did have my attention, but I tried not to think much of it. The same red bird from before was there; I'd seen it a few times, though I hadn't heard anyone else talk about it. I assumed it was part of my own hallucination. Every day after class, it came to the window of my bedroom, staring at me, chirping at me, taunting me. Forcing me to question myself. I learned to let it be, throwing my blanket over my head and thinking nothing of it; but it wouldn't leave me alone.

"Oh wow! It's beautiful. I've never seen one like that," Fane said. "You hardly see those things anymore. Well, that's what my parents say." He waited for a reply, but I only glanced at him.

He could see it, too? I adjusted myself in my seat.

"You're talking about the bird?" I asked, looking at him.

"What else could I be talking about?" Fane chuckled. "So, this is how I can get you to talk."

I sank down in my seat, letting my knees tilt closer to my chest. So what if Fane saw it, too? I was tired of chasing a ghost. Who cared if there was something beyond the desert? What was I going to do about it? I would end up in a worse place than Lukenic's special program. I just wished the bird, hallucination or not, would go away and leave me alone.

"Who said I was here because of my grandfather?" I asked, changing the subject.

"I have ears in high places, let's just say that. It makes sense why you haven't heard anything about being able to leave, even after three months of being here. Being raised by someone as mistrusted as him always takes a big toll. Even with signs of improvement, the administration might not be confident that you're rehabilitated."

"How do you even know that?" I asked.

He chuckled, keeping the same smile. "Well, my situation is similar to yours, and I've been here awhile … so yeah."

"How long?"

Fane laid his head back, glaring at the ceiling. "Over three years now. Hmm. Yep, something like that. And in three years, I've never seen anyone be here any longer than six months."

"Three years?"

"Yes. I don't like talking about it, but let's just say that my parents were very powerful people. Because they had different ideas that weren't popular, I was taken from them, and they were put away in a similar place like this for adults. They were my parents, so I shared their beliefs. They have to fix me and correct any thinking my parents might have instilled in me. I'm not here because of something I did, but what my parents did."

My eyes moved to an empty corner. The thought of not seeing my family for three years made me feel hopeless.

"Do you know when you get to leave?" I asked.

"No, I really don't."

"Why don't you just run away, then?"

"Why would I do that? This isn't a bad place; they just want to help me. They want to see that I will have an adult life that's not cluttered with nonsense. Could you imagine being in your grandfather's place? Is that the type of life you see for yourself? Locked up and imprisoned?"

"No," I said, feeling my chest flutter.

"Then you should understand more than anyone why this is for your well-being. Everyone knows what your grandfather was into. I'm just surprised it took this long before they stopped him. Perhaps what your grandfather believed wasn't considered too much of a threat since it was based on children's stories."

Fane continued to talk, but I hardly heard a word. I could only think of my grandfather.

I was happy with Grandpa before all of this. I was hardly ever sad when he and I were together, but I'd felt nothing but sadness since he was taken. The best thing that had ever happened to me was when I found out that I got to live with my grandpa while my parents were doing their research. I remembered that, even before I'd lived with him, he would tell me about stars, and I would draw pictures of how I thought they looked. He was really my best friend, way before I ever met Rita. And now it was like he wasn't even alive.

"Look at that. That's something," Fane said. He was looking down at the windowsill. The red bird was standing there, picking through its feathers. "I never saw a bird this close before," Fane said. "I think he's looking at you, Mae."

It did seem that way. For a moment, we didn't say a word, only watched the little cardinal. Right when I expected it to fly away, it didn't, just continued looking in my direction.

"Maybe it means something," Fane said. "Maybe it means things are about to turn around for you."

"There you are!" Avery said. I pivoted to see her walking toward me. She took a few confused glances at Fane. "I thought you were in your room?"

"She decided to come out and get some fresh air," Fane said. Avery narrowed her eyes as Fane smiled back at her.

"Why were you looking for me?" I asked.

"So, I guess you're talking now?" Avery looked slightly out of breath. "I need to talk to you." She glanced at Fane, then me. "Alone."

I followed Avery upstairs. I was a little taken aback that she needed to go all the way up to our room just to talk. What could be so important that she could only share it with me in private, right at that moment? As we entered our room, she looked down the hall to be sure that no one was nearby, and then she closed the door. I sat on my bed, pulling my feet up to cross my legs. She proceeded to look out our window toward the other side of campus.

"I don't trust that guy," Avery stated.

"Fane?"

"Yes."

"But I thought you liked him."

"Yeah, he's attractive, but he creeps me out. Walking around the way he does."

"He's just a student, Avery."

"Whatever. That doesn't change the fact that he's a creep."

"What's going on?" I asked.

"Your friend Rita," Avery started quietly as she walked over to me. "She said it was urgent and that she needed to talk to you."

"About what?"

"I don't know. She didn't tell me anything. She only said she needed to talk to you urgently. I think something happened to your parents."

Twenty Three

I followed Avery to the broken gate that led to the other side of campus. Rita did have outside contact, unlike me. I couldn't really think of what kind of bad news she would have heard—but I was scared. Since I had been here at Lukenic, I hadn't heard anything from my parents. I knew I wasn't allowed to contact them, but why hadn't my parents tried to contact me? I had assumed it was because of the bad way we had left things, but maybe it was something more.

It was starting to become evening, and the orange clouds grew dark, foreshadowing rain. Once we were on the other side, Avery put her hood over her head and headed to Kaleen's dorm. There was an after-school activity happening, so most of the students were indoors. A few security guards were on watch, but they paid no attention to us. I noticed Kaleen outside of the dorm talking to some other students. Once she saw us, she said goodbye to her friends and headed inside. Kaleen gave me a welcoming smile as we followed her.

"Just go up to my room. I'll be there shortly," Kaleen said as she turned down the hall.

Once there, I took a seat on the sofa, and Avery sat on the one across from me. I fumbled with my hands, waiting for Kaleen to return.

"Are you okay?" Avery asked. I wasn't looking up at her, but I could feel she was watching me.

"Yes, I'm fine."

"So why have you been shutting everyone out lately?" I knew I would have to answer this question from Avery eventually, but I really didn't want anyone to know about my situation. How stupid could I have been to believe that most people were brainwashed, except for me and Grandpa? Maybe I ignored what everyone told me because I wanted something to believe in.

"It's because of my grandfather," I started. "I saw him a few weeks ago."

"You did? How?"

"My cousin Marty took me to see him. We told the school I had an appointment, but we lied."

"Really?" Avery said. "It can't have been that easy."

"Well, I don't know how it worked, but I was able to go."

"That's interesting. How did your visit go?"

"He wasn't in good shape. He wasn't the same person anymore. It was very painful to see him."

"I'm sure that's true," Avery said, sliding her shoes to the floor to pull her legs together on the sofa. "I knew there had to be more to why you changed. He's in an institution; of course, he isn't himself."

"What else can I say? The man I saw wasn't the person I knew."

"Well, you don't have to say anything. We were becoming friends, so don't find it weird that I was worried about you, Mae."

"I thought you didn't want friends."

"Yeah, well, then take it as a compliment."

"Oh, okay." A small smile made its way to my lips. "Thank you."

A little bit later, Kaleen came through the door with Rita following.

"Mae?" Rita called as her eyes caught mine. I rose from my seat with my hands clenched together, my palms sweating.

"Hey," Rita said as she took a few steps forward. She looked eager to see me, but the memories of our last meeting flooded back in my mind.

"So, what's going on?" I said, looking away from her.

"Well," Rita started. She looked at Avery and Kaleen. "I don't know if you want other people around while we talk."

"Oh, of course." Kaleen moved toward another room. "You guys can talk in the bedroom, no problem."

"No," I said, stopping Kaleen in her tracks. "You can tell me here. They're my friends." I made sure to look Rita in the eyes when I said that.

"I'm—I'm sorry!" Rita cried, taking a step back. Her voice softened, suddenly becoming like a little girl's. "You, more than anyone, know how badly I wanted to be here at Lukenic. I just—" Rita fumbled over her words, but before she could say anything, I cut her off.

"You just thought it was important to distance yourself from me because you were afraid that just being friends with me could get you kicked out. Right?"

"It's not liked that, Mae. Why can't you understand?"

"I understand. Once you realized how people really viewed my family, you changed."

Rita's eyes widened, becoming glossy. All my anger was built up. I never got to tell her how I felt. I didn't care if she was hurt, but a part of me didn't want to see her cry. "You're supposed to be my friend,

Rita," I said, trying to bring my tone down. "And you treated me how everyone else did." There was cold silence between us. I could tell Avery and Kaleen were confused.

"Look, I didn't come here for this," Rita said as she turned to leave.

"Wait." Kaleen ran over to stop her. "You came here to tell Mae something important. You can't just leave. Regardless of whatever you guys are going through, if you have something important to tell her, you should."

Rita paused at the door, then turned back around. "Fine, I will." She stayed by the door, keeping space between us. "Since you don't care if anyone hears, I will just say it. Your father's in jail."

"What?"

"Everyone is talking about it. It happened almost a week ago. My mom told me that it was your mother who reported him."

"Reported him! Reported him for what? My dad doesn't do anything wrong!"

"I don't know, I think it was something to do with what he was researching, something against the law."

"You're lying. Mom wouldn't do that to my dad."

"I'm not! Why would I lie about that? Do you think I hate you or something?" Rita shouted.

I took a few steps toward her. "My mother would never do something like that," I said, making it clear I didn't trust her anymore.

"Fine, don't believe me!" Rita said. She turned away, leaving the room.

I stayed in the same place Rita left me. I was still trying to process what she'd said. I grabbed ahold of the side of my neck as I felt the Abnormal irritating my skin. The same burning I'd felt before.

"I didn't expect that," Avery started.

"Oh, Mae, I'm sorry," Kaleen said, coming over to hug me. I let my head rest on her shoulder. The tears came again, but this time I didn't try to hold them back. "I have to go. I can't stay here anymore. I have to go home," I sobbed.

"And how are you going to do that?" Avery said.

I raised my head up from Kaleen, wiping away my tears. "I don't know, but I am," I replied as I walked over to the sofa.

"Well, you can't leave this place unless you just walk out right in front of security; otherwise, it's not going to happen," Avery added.

"I don't know, but maybe I can help," Kaleen said, sitting next to me.

"Even if you can, how is that going to help Mae?" Avery protested.

"Well, as a member of a mentorship program for younger students who will be attending Lukenic in the future, I have access to a vehicle. We had a group of students that came last week and are supposed to leave tonight after the party we're throwing for them. I volunteered to give some of them a ride home."

"So, you're going to put Mae in your trunk and sneak her out?"

"Nope, even better. I'll say she's one of the students. She still looks young enough to pass."

"You would do that for me?" I said, turning to Kaleen. "But what if we get caught? You could get in trouble."

"Well, this is important. Besides, I did say I was a fan of your grandfather. It would be an honor to help his granddaughter. You're just as brilliant as he is, I'm sure."

"You really think my grandfather is brilliant?"

"Yes, and I'm the top student at Lukenic, so that has to count for something. I'm the one who started the Niles Cefend Fan Base and Strange Phenomenon Club. Although you guys aren't members, I can trust you, and even my sister, although she thinks I'm crazy."

"You are crazy. You're really going to risk getting caught to take Mae home?"

"Yes," Kaleen responded with a smile. "And that's if we get caught."

"Okay, then I'm coming, too," Avery said.

"You are?" Kaleen said.

"Why not? It sounds fun."

"Well, I don't know how you would pass as a middle schooler—plus, security knows your face."

"Then you can stick me in the trunk."

"Whatever," Kaleen said, rolling her eyes at Avery. "Meet me here in my dorm tonight at eleven-thirty p.m. We will leave at midnight. I'm pretty sure this will be the only night that would work, so don't be late."

Kaleen walked us out of the dorm. Before we left, I pulled her aside.

"I need to tell you something," I said. Avery saw us, but she didn't interrupt.

"What is it?"

I threw my arms around her. "Thanks for helping me. I never met anyone like you before." Kaleen wrapped her arms around me how Mom used to before she changed. She squeezed me tight, rocking side to side.

"I told you, Mae, it really is an honor." I hadn't known her long, but I was overwhelmed by who she was. Just being around her put a spark in my heart.

The rain had started to fall as Avery and I headed back to our side of campus. We knew curfew was ending soon, so we moved through the bushes quickly. Avery stepped out of the broken fence, taking my hand to help me through.

"AHA!" a voice from behind us said as we came out of the bushes.

"Funny finding you two here." When we turned around, Fane stood there with two security guards at his sides.

"So, this is where you been hiding, Avery. And you decided to bring Mae with you this time."

Twenty Four

The security guards had taken hold of Avery and me before we knew it. Avery fought back, thrashing and screaming, as I tried to slip quietly from their grip.

"I knew it!" Avery yelled as the guards pulled us away. "I knew that asshole wasn't a student!"

"Not a student?" I shouted. I looked back as the guard took me away, and the rain began falling harder. Fane stood there with his hands in his pockets, watching us being dragged away. He slowly shook his head at me.

The guards took us to the dormitory, but through the back. They covered our mouths with their hands to keep us from yelling. Once inside, they carried us up several flights of stairs. Avery kept fighting by grabbing the staircase rails to make them fall backward. My guard noticed that Avery was not letting up, so he threw me over his shoulder and began to run up the stairs. Separated from them, I could now only hear Avery struggling—that is, until I heard a whacking sound followed by a body hitting the ground. My heart began to race; I couldn't hear Avery's voice anymore.

Finally, we reached a small, empty room. The guard pulled out his handcuffs, securing me to a bar that stuck out of the wall and reached from one side of the room to another. After I was locked, he left to help the other guard. The bar had blockers that kept me in place, so I couldn't slide side to side. Its low level meant I was sitting on the ground. Moments later, the second guard came in with Avery unconscious in his arms, and the other guard followed behind. He laid her on the other side of the room and cuffed her to the same bar. On the side of her head, her mask was torn open and her face was swollen. She only moved slightly as she tried to open her eyes.

"Avery," I called. She tried looking at me, but she was too weak. The guards left the room, locking the door behind them. I tried to wiggle my hands through the handcuffs to see if it was possible to get loose, but they were too tight. I screamed in frustration, pulling and kicking at the pole. And then the tears started. First, I learned my father was arrested because of my mother, and now this. I didn't care anymore about anything. I just wanted my old life back. How could Fane do this to us? Fane had made himself seem like a friend, someone who wanted to help me. I could finally see the heartless and untrustworthy person he was.

Eventually, I wore myself out trying to get free, and collapsed to the ground.

"It's not going to work," Avery said in her weak voice. "They brought me here on my first day. You're just wasting your energy." One of her eyes was swelling up.

"Avery?" I cried. "Are you okay?"

Avery rolled her head over to the wall, resting it there. "No," she replied. "I can't believe they hit me."

"What's going to happen to us?" I asked, but she didn't respond. She only closed her eyes. There was a window above us, but we were locked up too low to look out of it. What now? I wanted to yell for help, but I was afraid that the guards would come back and do to me what they did to Avery.

I looked around the room, trying to find something to pick the handcuffs, but there wasn't anything. The room was cold, and being wet from the rain only made it colder. I called Avery's name again but got no response. I really hoped there wasn't something seriously wrong with her. I called her name for a third time, and a few moments later she responded.

"What?" Avery said sluggishly.

"Just checking that you're still alive. You don't look good," I said.

"I knew Fane was a class model," Avery said drowsily.

"What do you mean?" I asked. "What's a class model?"

"Fane," she replied. "Some classes in Lukenic have a class model. It's someone the school uses to set a good example of how they want us to act." Avery took a deep breath as she tried pulling herself up. "They usually get someone attractive, a goody-goody. Someone who would be popular enough that the other students would want to follow."

"So, Fane isn't a student?" I asked.

"Nope, just some young guy they paid to keep us under control. I honestly didn't think they would put one here for us, but I guess it makes sense. You usually don't know they're a class model until you get in trouble. They're pretty much the ears of the school. Reporting everything the students do."

"I guess that makes sense now."

"I should have known. I've been in Lukenic ever since I was five."

It was twenty minutes before someone came to our room. When the door opened, Fane appeared, closing it behind him. He pulled up a chair to sit in front of us. He sat backward and rested his chin on the top of it. He let out a big sigh.

"I'm so disappointed in you guys, especially you, Mae," Fane started. "I'm not that surprised about you, Avery. This is supposed to be a place to help you guys grow and become better students, children, adults, and most importantly, citizens. I knew you were a troublemaker, Miss. Avery Roman, but I really couldn't imagine you leaving to go to the other side. You know, there are cameras everywhere. You think that we wouldn't check them to figure out where you were disappearing to?"

"Took you long enough," Avery snarled.

"So, you really aren't a student," I interrupted.

"I used to be a student here. But now I have finished this program, and I am a better person."

"So, you're a liar! You tried to get close to me by lying."

"I didn't lie about everything. The reason I'm here wasn't a lie. I really thought I could share some things about myself with you in hopes that you would take my advice. I told you to not get involved with Avery, and now look where you are."

"So now what?" Avery asked.

"Well, I contacted Ms. Vivly and Mr. Owns. They will be handling what will happen to you both. Though, I can tell you that you will not be here at Lukenic, but somewhere much worse. Probably similar to the place where your grandfather is, Mae. Did you get a good look at that place?" Fane said, tilting his head with a smirk.

"You knew I went to see him?" I asked.

"Of course. Like I said before, I have ears in high places. The funny thing is that you actually thought we would let you leave this campus not knowing where you were going. Oh, we knew. If you really needed to see a doctor, someone here could have taken you. We only allowed you to see your grandfather as part of your rehabilitation. Your cousin Marty reported to us about how badly you wanted to see him. We thought it was a good idea for you to see where your grandfather ended up because of the things he taught you. But I guess that didn't work. You're still being rebellious."

Fane lifted his head from his arms. He had no emotion, and the look in his eyes was soulless. Any ounce of affection I felt for him was gone.

"And your cousin Marty told us all about your hallucinations. Your grandfather talked about stars, and now you're seeing them, too. That's the real reason you're here, so you can't spread your insanity to the other people in your community. There was never any intention for you to leave this place until you turned twenty." He chuckled. "That's right, Avery. Your friend is crazier than her grandfather. We thought since you were so young, there was time to help you, Mae. But I guess not. Don't blame Marty he was just trying to help you."

I kept my eyes on the floor. I had no thoughts. I wanted to wake up from this nightmare. I flashed back to my family when I was younger, before my parents were gone all the time, when they fought less and Grandpa's reputation wasn't so bad. The world had been simple. I thought about my dad coming into my room to wake me up, and my mom in her office working. I imagined Grandpa sitting in the living room, reading while smoking his pipe. I didn't want to imagine what was to come next for me, in reality.

"I'm sorry, Mae," Fane said as he rose and headed for the door. "I was really rooting for you."

Twenty Five

"I guess this is it," Avery said, trying to keep her body upright. "We are probably going to an institution. My parents will probably let them take me this time."

"I'm sure my parents don't have a say in the matter, especially since Dad's in jail. They sent me here, but I know they didn't want to. At least I hope they didn't."

"This place is sick," Avery said. "They let you see your grandpa as part of your rehabilitation. Are you serious? No wonder you came back totally different."

"It wasn't really seeing him that changed me," I replied. "It was when I realized that I couldn't tell the difference between what was real and what was just my imagination. It was when I realized I couldn't trust my own mind. Everything I saw, everything I heard. The things I felt, inside and outside of my body. I couldn't trust if they were real."

I lay on the floor on my side with my back facing the door. My cuffed wrist hung over my body, and I stared at the dust that had settled under the bar. There were four more spaces to put a handcuff through. I didn't want to think about anything anymore. I closed my eyes, hoping that when I woke up, I would be back home in my room. But I didn't sleep.

It was getting dark outside and in the room, so my other senses began to turn on. I heard the sound of footsteps echoing in the room above, and voices. It seemed like there was a lot happening up there. Then, suddenly, all the noise stopped. I tried to think of what room it could be, but I didn't even know what floor I was on. The room grew darker, and only the red lights outside that lit up campus shined through.

Desperate for something to focus on, I noticed something small that looked like a pin under the bar to the back of the wall. I rose to get a better look. Was it really a pin? I tried to see if I could reach it as I slid off my shoes and tried to use my toes to touch it.

"What are you doing?" Avery asked, resting her head on the wall.

"I think I see a pin," I said as I tried to shove my foot under the bar. I felt the pin on my toe and began to pull it toward me. "Got it."

"Give it to me. I know how to pick a lock," Avery said. I tried to grab it with my toes, and once I did, I tossed it in Avery's direction. It was close enough that Avery could use her foot to pull it closer. She used her teeth to pick it up and put the pin in her hands. As soon as she started to pick at her handcuffs, an alarm went off in the hall.

"What's that?" I said, jumping from the sound. Avery was startled, too, dropping the pin on the ground.

"No," she cried as she tried to find it.

"Sounds like the fire alarm," I said. And it wasn't long before we smelled smoke. "Is someone going to come for us?" I asked.

Avery managed to find the pin.

She picked it up and worked on her handcuffs again.

"I don't know what's happening, but I'm not going to wait," Avery said as she moved the pin to release her handcuffs. It felt like it was taking forever. Smoke began to filter through our air vents.

Then Avery's handcuff clicked open. She pulled her cuff from the bar and headed toward me. The smoke started to fill the room, making it hard to breathe. Some minutes later, I was finally released, and we both ran to the door, but it was locked.

The hallway was filled with smoke. We banged and screamed for help as the smoke filled the room, making it hard to see each other. I collapsed to the ground, trying to breathe; Avery tried her best to stay up, calling for help. Then someone from the other side banged against the door. Over and over again. "Avery, Mae." Theo's voice was on the other side. "Get out of the way." And with one more bang, Theo busted through the door with Dime.

Avery was able to crawl from the room as Theo carried me out.

"Let's get out of here," he said, heading towards the back staircase. We all ran down the stairs and headed outside. We could see that the security guards were running around, panicking. Avery told us to follow her as she tried to catch her breath. Theo put me on his back, and we headed to the broken gate that led back to the other side of Lukenic. We stayed in the bushes watching everything before making our next move.

"So, do you guys like my escape plan?" Theo said.

"What escape plan?" Avery said.

"I started the fire."

"You what?" Avery and I both shouted.

"Are you crazy? We could have died," I said, coughing.

"We were handcuffed." Avery raised her arm and took ahold of mine, showing Theo our wrists with cuffs hanging.

"Oh." Theo paused. "Well, it worked out, didn't it?"

"So, how did you guys know we needed to be rescued?" Avery asked.

"We heard you guys in the room below us, plus Dime saw the guards take you. Dime did all the brainstorming," Theo explained.

"It wasn't my idea to start the fire," Dime responded.

"Yeah, but he was the one who noticed something was wrong, and we could hear you guys through the air vents talking to that asshole Fane. I think our room is right above the one you guys were in."

"Well, the fire was a good distraction," Avery replied. "But I'm sure they're going to realize we're all gone soon."

"Or burned alive," Theo said.

"So, we better make a plan quick." Avery pulled out the pin and started working on her other handcuffed wrist.

"We already have a plan," I realized, excited. "We can still escape with your sister!"

"Oh, yeah, that's right!"

"Escape? You two already made plans to leave? Without including us?" Theo said.

"It's not like that," I said. "We decided to run just before we got caught."

"Caught doing what?" Dime chimed in.

"Sneaking over to the other side of campus," I replied.

Avery's handcuff was open, and she started to work on my other cuffed wrist.

"You two have been sneaking to the other side of campus?" Theo asked.

"Yeah," Avery replied.

"And you never told us?" Theo almost shouted.

"It would have been too risky, Theo. The only reason we are

escaping is to get Mae home to see what happened to her parents."

"Well, I'm coming, too. Right, Dime?" Theo said, looking at his partner in crime.

"We already burned the school down. What do we have to lose?" Dime said in a nonchalant tone.

"I don't know if Kaleen is going to be able to get us all out of here," I said.

"Well, she has to know," Avery said. "This idiot burned down the building."

"Seriously," Theo said, looking like he was losing his patience. "I was trying to help."

"Okay, we'll figure it all out once we get to her dorm," I said.

Once Avery was done with my cuffs, we headed to the other side of campus. A lot of the students were outside watching the fire from afar. It was a better distraction than we thought. Kaleen had given Avery the card to get into the building in case we didn't have someone to follow inside. We walked through without being noticed. With two boys walking in the girls' dorm room, I was sure it would cause a problem, but the halls were empty. We headed straight to Kaleen's room. Avery pulled out the key from her shoe to let us in and quickly closed the door.

"Huh, who are these guys?" Kaleen said, standing in front of her window and looking at us.

"They're running with us," Avery said. "This is Theo and Dime. Theo and Dime, this is Kaleen, my twin sister."

"Running? I don't know if I can take this many people without any issues," Kaleen said.

"Well, they're the ones who started the fire, so you have to help them."

"What?"

"You said you wanted an adventure, Kaleen. Now you have one."

"This was supposed to be about helping Mae. What happened that you guys had to start a fire?!"

"I'm really sorry, Kaleen," I began as I walked over to her. I could imagine it was overwhelming. "When we got back to the other side of Lukenic, we got caught," I explained. "They knocked Avery unconscious and locked her and me in a room. They were going to send us to a worse institution, like the place where they sent my grandpa. So, Theo and Dime helped us escape." Kaleen looked at Avery and saw the gash on the side of her head.

"Oh, my goodness!" Kaleen said as she walked over to Avery to examine her head. She reached out to touch her wound.

"I'm fine," Avery replied, yanking her head away.

We heard the fire truck sirens coming toward the school. And from Kaleen's big window, we could see more students and staff heading outside to look at the fire.

"I guess if we're going to leave, this will be the best time. The car is parked in the back of this building. If we hurry, maybe no one will notice us."

Kaleen grabbed a couple of things before she headed to the door. Before leaving her room, she looked down the hall to be sure no one was there. She signaled us to follow, and we did. She took us to the end of the hall to the back stairs, which were hardly used. Once we reached the first floor, Kaleen took another look outside the door before we made our exit. She gave us a signal, and we headed to the back of the building, where the car was parked.

The fire on the other side of Lukenic had grown bigger than before. We could feel the heat. We reached the car and saw, over the wall, that more fire trucks were coming. "Mae, you sit in the passenger's seat; and Dime, you sit behind me. That way they can see I have kids with me. And you two," Kaleen said, pointing at Theo and Avery. "Try to look small; you have to pass as fifth graders." She pulled out a blanket from her trunk and laid it over their legs. "And pretend that you're asleep; maybe they won't ask any questions."

Kaleen started the car, and we drove off to the gate. As we pulled up, there was one guard standing outside his booth watching the fire. He walked over to us. "Hello, Miss Kaleen. Taking some students home tonight?"

"Yup, I sure am," Kaleen said.

"It seems pretty early. I thought you all were having a party tonight before they left. Did it get canceled?" the guard said.

I glanced back at everyone. Theo and Avery pretended to be asleep. Avery sat in the middle between Dime and Theo, laying her head on Theo's shoulder, and Theo laid his head against his window. Dime just sat quietly staring ahead as the guard looked back at him.

"I don't know if the party got canceled; I was just told these guys were ready to get back home."

"Well, I got a report that some students are loose from the program over there, and that they started the fire."

"Really! That's crazy," Kaleen said, trying to look shocked.

"Yeah, so I have to look in everyone's car that's leaving tonight."

"Well, I don't have anyone but the students I've been looking after this week."

"Well, then you won't mind if I take a look."

"Of course not," Kaleen said as she looked worriedly at me.

The guard walked to the back seat, where Dime was sitting, and shined his flashlight at him.

"I didn't realize our visitor students were wearing our school uniform."

"It's a souvenir," Kaleen said.

The guard walked to Theo's side and pointed his flashlight in his face.

"Him, too."

"Yes, why not?" Kaleen said.

"He doesn't look like a grade-school kid to me with that facial hair."

"Wait," Kaleen said in a panic, opening her door.

"Miss. Kaleen, please stay in the car," the guard said as he tapped on Theo's window with his flashlight. "Wake up, kid, and step out of the car."

Theo raised his head and did what the guard said. The guard pulled out his walkie-talkie, but before he could use it, Theo took the guard out with one blow to the face. The guard hit the ground, unmoving. Theo jumped into the car, closed the door, and shouted to Kaleen, "Go, go, go!"

"What did you just do?" Kaleen shouted in a panic.

"Kaleen, drive!" Avery shouted.

"Oh, my goodness!" Kaleen said as she slammed the door and pulled off quickly.

"I can't believe you just did that!" Kaleen yelled, her hands tightly gripping the steering wheel. She fixated on the road, speeding as fast as she could. "We are in so much trouble."

"Forget it, Kaleen, and just drive," Avery shouted. We knew Theo could be impulsive, but never thought he would punch a guard; there was no turning back now. My heart was like a sledgehammer in my chest as I kept hoping we weren't being followed. I looked at Kaleen, wondering if she regretted helping me now. Even though it was Theo who had made things worse, I couldn't help but blame myself.

"I'm sorry," I said to Kaleen. But she didn't respond immediately.

She took a deep breath and straightened. "So, tell me how to get to your house."

Twenty Six

It was about a forty-five-minute ride to my house. There was silence for most of it. Dime had managed to fall asleep, though the rest of us were wide-awake. I wasn't sure how someone could sleep in the situation we were in, but I guessed burning the school down had taken a lot out of him.

"Now that you all are runaways, what are you going to do?" Kaleen said.

"Ha, shouldn't you be asking yourself that question? You're one of us now, Kaleen."

"I'll figure everything out for myself. I'm not the one with the bad reputation. They probably think I was forced into helping you guys."

"I don't know what I'm going to do," Theo said. "But I can't go back home. My family is already ashamed of me."

"What for?" Avery asked.

"Because I'm out of control," Theo started. "My emotions get the best of me. I told you before, my father's a judge and he thinks my behavior jeopardizes his position. A judge has to have an orderly home to be qualified. So, he sent me to the other side, while my brothers are his proud trophies. So, yeah."

"That's terrible," Kaleen said.

"That's nothing. You know why Dime is here? Former President Cape is Dime's grandfather. His youngest daughter fell for one of the servants and got pregnant. So, when Dime was born, he was sent away to be with his father's family. His dad was paid to keep quiet about his relationship with Dime's mother. When Dime's father died, Dime became a burden on his father's family. The family threatened to expose Dime's mother if the president didn't give them money. When President Cape found out, he had the family executed."

"They killed his family!" I almost shouted.

"Dime's mother begged him not to hurt her son. So, President Cape took custody of Dime so that he could have better control over him. And when he did, he sent Dime to Lukenic to keep him out of the way." When Theo finished, the car fell silent. It started to make sense why Dime was so distant. I could see how close Theo and Dime had become. Theo looked like Dime's older brother as he rested on Theo's shoulder.

"I wonder what Fane's story is," I said.

"Who cares? That guy's a traitor!" Avery said. "Whatever comes out of that jerk's mouth can't be trusted. Nothing he says is genuine."

"I was just wondering," I said. "Regardless of what he did, he's like us in a way."

"How?" Avery demanded.

"Well, he's young like us. If he hadn't been broken by the school administration, I'm sure he would be like us, too."

"Fane has no family," Theo said. "He was taken from them,

because of some crime against Eradeem. I don't know what crime, though."

"How do you know that?" Avery said.

"We used to live in the same neighborhood. Plus, my dad was the judge that separated them," Theo replied.

"Fane was telling me something like that earlier today," I said.

"Well, everyone knows why I'm here," Avery said. "But what about you, Mae? First you told me you were here because you got caught trying to leave Eradeem, then Fane says you're here because you see hallucinations."

I took a deep breath, resting my head on the car window. I wanted to forget everything regarding Grandpa, stars, and Lev. Running away from Lukenic was kind of a relief from having to think about all of that.

"I guess leaving Eradeem was the hallucination and everything else I said that happened," I started. "I don't really know anything anymore. I don't know if anything I told you really happened to me. All I know is that something is wrong with me. I feel like I've been lied to my whole life by my grandfather."

"No way that's true," Kaleen interrupted. "Your grandfather is a brilliant man, Mae. He was brave and courageous. I mean, I never heard of a man so confident in what he believed."

"I don't really want to talk about him, or anything right now," I said, stopping Kaleen from continuing.

It wasn't long after our short conversation ended that we pulled up to my driveway. I sat there in the passenger seat for a moment before I realized I was finally home. I didn't remember the area being as dark as it was. It was one of the most remote houses in Eradeem. I'd been away from home for three months, so maybe that was it. But still, something didn't feel right. The reality of why I was here started to sink in. My father wasn't here anymore. Not because he was off doing research. He was arrested because of my mother.

I was really hoping that whatever happened may have somehow worked itself out and that my father would be in there. But if he wasn't, what then? I wanted an explanation from my mother. I wanted to know what kind of wife betrayed her husband who had only been good to the family. It didn't matter what wrong he had done; betrayal was the worst kind of sin against your family. I stayed pinned to my seat, staring at the dashboard, wondering if maybe we all could run away together.

"Are you okay?" Theo asked.

"I don't know."

"If you want, I can go inside with you," Theo said. Looking back at Theo, I nodded. Avery reached from behind me, placing her hand on my knee to stop it from shaking.

"I'll come, too, if you want," she said.

I opened my door and stepped out of the car. Theo and Avery followed me to my front door. I turned the knob before I knocked, and it opened without force. The whole house was dark, but it looked the way it always had. Books and paper cluttered the space. My mother usually stayed up pretty late, but there was no sign of her.

"Hello?" I called as I stepped inside. I saw a light on upstairs to the left, coming from the direction of my parents' room. I was sure they would be shocked to see me, but I hoped they would be happy, too. I heard the door gently close behind me.

I switched on the living room light. "Mom?" I motioned for the others to wait as I made my way up the stairs, treading as lightly as possible so I wouldn't startle anyone. Once I made it to the top, I noticed the bathroom light was on and the door wide open. The floor was covered in pieces of mask; makeup was all over the sink, and shiny silver shards the size of coins were everywhere.

"What *is* this?" They were like scales from a fish or a reptile. I stooped to examine them, and then I heard a sound. I jumped up and turned toward my parents' room. I stepped into the hall and saw a trail of the scales down it. My heart felt like a hammer against my chest as I made my way toward what I could tell was heavy breathing. Peeking through the cracked door of my parents' bedroom, I could see someone was there. To open the door wider would make too much noise. If it was my mom, if she was hurt, I did not want to scare her.

"Mom?"

There, sitting on the edge of the bed with their back completely exposed, was someone I didn't recognize. They had blotches of the shiny stuff from the bathroom all over their skin. If this was some type of Abnormal, I had never seen anything like it before. It didn't really look like something a mask could cover. They were weeping. I walked toward them and called out for my mother one last time. I was close enough to reach out and touch them, but before I did, a voice—no, a dry whisper— called out to me.

"Mae." It was a hoarse, deep voice I didn't recognize. The thing looked over their shoulder at me, and I staggered backward in horror. Their nose was crumbling away, the flesh of their face sinking into the bones—half skin, half scales. They formed their lips to speak again but began to cough uncontrollably, turning away. I rushed around the bed to comfort them. I hesitated, taking their hands in mine. My body reacted before I knew what was happening. I could not let go. "Mom!" I called it. I couldn't recognize this as my mother, but their eye...they were my mother's small, honey-brown eyes. "What happened to you?" I said, falling to my knees in front of her. What I saw was frightening, but love for my mother kept me from running.

I reached out to touch her face and, as I did, she grabbed hold of my wrist, pulling me away. Her grip was strong and her thick nails dug into my skin.

"Leave. You need to leave, Mae," she cried. Her voice changed again, but this time it was more monstrous. She was a woman trapped inside of a creature.

I pulled from her grip as she let me go. "Mom, I'm going to go get help, okay?"

I ran out of the room. The creature cried out, and I could hear my mother's voice through the creature screaming. My mind was scrambled as I pulled the door closed behind me. Suddenly a loud crash and a scream came from the room. I felt heat coming from the door as a bright yellow glow flowed through the bottom of the doorframe. Crackling and the sound of something breaking came through the door.

"Mae!" Avery shouted from downstairs. "Are you okay? What was that?"

I didn't respond because I didn't know the answer. I reached for the doorknob; but, as I did, I jumped back. The knob had burned me. "Mom!" I cried as I kicked at the door.

After the third kick, the door swung open, and what I saw would haunt me in my sleep. The room was a total blaze of fire. Everything that could catch on fire had. And in the middle of my parents' bedroom was a beast standing on all fours. It had a long neck, thick tail, large teeth, and a lizard-like head; it filled half of the room. It took a step toward me as its tail swung, smashing the windows. Everything in me was screaming at me to run, but my body was paralyzed. Everything seemed to move in slow motion, and it was becoming harder to breathe. I couldn't tell if it was because of the fear that was gripping me or the smoke that surrounded me.

The thing took another step toward me, pulling its neck back and opening its mouth. A bright yellow glow appeared and grew from its throat. Before I realized what was happening, I could feel someone taking my arm and pulling me back, and my legs followed. "Run, Avery, run!" Theo yelled.

Theo pulled me down the stairs and, with a quick jerk, made a sharp turn into our living room, falling on the floor. Flames barreled down the stairs, setting half of the living room on fire. Avery was on the other side of the house screaming as the beast made its way down the stairs, collapsing to the ground. As it rose, it looked at Theo and me. Right before charging in our direction, it made a loud, monstrous sound. Both Theo and I ducked, covering our heads and hoping that we wouldn't be killed.

Once I realized I wasn't dead, I looked up, and I could see outside. The beast had broken through the wall and charged into the woods. The room grew dark as I watched the beast in the forest. For a moment, I thought I was being consumed by the fire. Perhaps I was being consumed by the smoke. I couldn't remember anything after that.

Twenty Seven

When I woke up, I was lying on a bed in a hospital room. I was hooked up to IVs with bandages on my arm. The window next to my bed was open. The sky was dark. I wasn't sure if it was the same day. I lifted myself up as pain from my bandaged arm shocked me. I screamed and fell back in the bed. I was still wearing my uniform from Lukenic, and parts of it were singed from fire.

Everything from the previous night rushed back to my mind. Were my friends okay? I tried to remember what had happened. I remembered Theo and Avery were in my house, and it was on fire. Then a beast had appeared. A fire-breathing beast. Did that all really happen? How was I still alive?

"Mom," I said, at first in a whisper. Her face flashed before me, and the tears fell. "Mom!" I cried out repeatedly. Just like I would after a horrible nightmare. Moments later, Mom would appear. She would take me in her arms, assure me that it was just a dream. But she wouldn't come this time. Instead, my aunt entered through the door. I felt my heart almost come out of my chest because, for a few seconds, I believed my aunt was her.

"Mae?" my aunt called to me. She walked over to my bed to embrace me. I'd never noticed how much she resembled my mother. She held me to her chest, rubbing my head and kissing my forehead. She let out a deep breath. My eyes stayed wide as tears continued to fill them and then fall. I was trying to hold off my thoughts, but my mouth opened against my will.

"Where's my mom?" I asked my aunt. "Is she okay?"

"I don't know," she said. "They're looking for her." The room fell quiet. My aunt loosened her arms. "You're safe now. You were rescued from that burning house. That's what matters right now."

"But the monster?" I said, pulling away from my aunt and staring her straight in her eyes. "That—that thing! What was it? Did it hurt my friends? Are they all right?"

"Monster?" my aunt said as she gave me a confused look. "Honey, what are you talking about?"

"The beast that burned the house down."

"Oh, honey. Your classmate, you mean. They took him to jail," she said.

I blinked a few times, trying to understand what she was saying to me. "No, no. Theo saved me," I protested.

"I don't know, hon, but he started the fire, just like he did at your school. Don't worry, they caught him."

"No!" I shouted. "It was a monster! It had fire coming from its mouth. It was in Mom's room. And it…" I stopped, looking away, trying to think. I was trying to understand how the monster came to be in my parents' room.

"Theo didn't set the fire," I said calmly as I searched my thoughts.

"Honey, do you need me to get the doctor?"

"No," I shouted. "Tell me what happened."

"Okay, I'm going to get the doctor." My aunt hurried out of the room.

What was going on? When she left, I removed the IVs from my arm, and everything else that was connected to me, and I got out of bed. I needed to find my friends. They'd been at my house. They'd seen the beast. Why didn't my aunt know about it? I stepped into the hall, looking around quietly. I could see my aunt to my left talking to a nurse. I went in the opposite direction, looking into rooms, hoping I would see Avery, Kaleen, Dime, or Theo. The first few rooms were empty. One room had someone with bandages wrapped around his head. I walked in.

"Theo," I called out.

"I'm sorry," he said. "You must have the wrong room."

"Oh, sorry," I said as I turned to leave. Walking back into the hall, I ran into a doctor.

"Miss Meadows," the doctor said. "Is everything okay?"

"I don't know," I replied.

"Well, come this way. I can explain everything. Let's go back to your room." The doctor took me by the hand and led me back. My aunt was standing in the hallway looking at me, pressing her hand against her chest. She came into the room as the doctor walked me in.

"Okay, let me examine you first," the doctor said. She pulled out a tool and shined a light into both of my eyes.

"So, what's going on? Where are my friends?" I asked.

"Everyone is fine. No one was badly injured. But I can't really say where they are. I do know the oldest boy is in jail."

"Why?" I demanded. "He didn't burn my house down; I'm trying to tell you it was some kind of beast."

The doctor just stared at me, adjusting her glasses. She looked at my aunt. "I was told she suffers from hallucinations. She got too close to some type of chemical, right?" the doctor said.

"Yes, that's what I was told," my aunt replied.

"Wait, no, I wasn't hallucinating. I mean…" I stopped myself, trying to think. "No, it was real, maybe. Maybe I…"

"Honey, you need to relax, okay? I will be right back." The doctor left me in the room with my aunt. My aunt came over and began rubbing my back, but I was disconnected from my surroundings and didn't hear anything she was saying. What was going to happen? I looked crazy in front of everyone. I was aware that what I was saying sounded impossible. Would they send me to an institution, the way Fane said they were going to before the fire started at Lukenic? My mind felt scrambled, and I wasn't sure what to believe. I knew if I kept talking about monsters, they would definitely put me in an institution. But maybe I did belong there.

The doctor came back with someone else. He wore a white coat like my doctor did, but something about his air made me wary of him. Before my doctor could introduce me, I spoke first. This time I made sure my tone was under control. "I'm sorry, I just realized I wasn't hallucinating. It was a dream I was having before I woke up," I said, putting on a fake chuckle. "I used to have hallucinations, but since I started at Lukenic, I haven't had that problem. I think I just woke up a bit disoriented."

"Oh," the other doctor said, looking at my aunt and then the new doctor. "She's probably suffering from a bit of trauma from the fire, which is giving her nightmares."

"Yes, I think so," I said. "Well, if you want, we can set up some therapy sessions."

"Oh, that sounds wonderful," my aunt said.

"I was told that a Ms. Vivly would be coming and taking you to a more proper place for your education," the doctor said.

"Right now?" I replied.

"Well, sometime today or tomorrow."

"I would feel more comfortable going home with my aunt, if possible."

"Well, that isn't my decision, but you can probably go home for now. You don't really need to be here anymore. I can contact Ms. Vivly and send her to get you from your aunt's home. When she comes, I'm sure you can discuss this with her."

I knew once Ms. Vivly showed up, there was no way I could convince her to let me stay with my aunt. I was sure she knew about Avery and me getting caught going to the other side of Lukenic. And, although I wasn't the one who'd started the school fire, I was sure I'd be considered a part of it. Theo had only started the fire to help us escape; and, on top of that, we had run away. The doctor probably didn't know all of those details. If he did, he wouldn't have let me go with my aunt.

As we arrived at her home, anxiety hit me deeply. It was just a matter of time before I would be taken away.

"What were you doing at your home last night, Mae? Were you not supposed to be a Lukenic?" my aunt asked.

I stood there at the front entry, feeling the uneasiness. "I was just trying to find out what happened to my dad. I was told he was in jail."

"Oh, did no one talk to you about that?" my aunt said. "Yeah, he was taken. It's getting crazy. First Grandpa, now your father. And who knows where your mother is." My aunt took a seat in the kitchen that wasn't too far from the entry.

"Do you know why Dad was put in jail?"

My aunt let out a huge sigh as she laid her arms on the kitchen table, slightly shaking her head. "I think your mother was afraid that your dad was getting into some research that he wasn't supposed to be involved in. She thought he would cause more trouble for the family. So she did what she thought was right, by turning him in."

There was silence in the room. I had no words for what my mother had done. Whatever my dad was up to, I couldn't imagine it being so bad that he would need to be arrested.

"You can have a seat, dear. Don't just stand there. You're making me worried."

"I'm scared," I confessed as I trembled.

"Honey, come here." My aunt reached for me like a mother to a child. But I wasn't a child anymore. At least, I knew I wouldn't be given the same privileges as a child when doing something wrong. I walked over to my aunt as she stood to hug me.

"Please don't let them take me away like they did Grandpa and my dad," I cried.

"Mae, nothing like that is going to happen to you."

"What if they took Mom, too?" I sobbed. My aunt didn't respond. She was probably thinking the same thing.

"Maybe you need to go upstairs and get a bit of rest, okay? Marty isn't home right now. He'll probably be out for a few days. You go to his room, okay?" my aunt said. "If you want to, Marcella is upstairs with her dad. You could stop by to say hi."

"Yeah, maybe I should," I replied. As I turned to leave, my aunt stopped me.

"I forgot something. Rita stopped by the hospital right before you woke up." My aunt reached into her purse and pulled out a white envelope. "I don't know what it is, but she said she thought you might have lost the first one you had." I took the envelope from my aunt. In it was a picture of Lev. The picture I had taken when he'd found me in the woods. I had forgotten all about it. I stood there looking at the photo. I rubbed my fingers against it. It felt real, I thought.

"What do you see in this picture?" I asked my aunt.

She leaned over, studying the distorted photo.

"It looks like a man blocking out the camera flash. Who is it?"

"It's a friend," I said.

Fear was lifted off me when she said that. I was about to be taken to a mental institution—or worse, to be executed, like Dime's family. For all I knew, that was going to happen to my whole family. Yet, suddenly, I felt a sense of peace. The picture was real, and the memories attached to it were real, too. The stars, the lanterns, and Lev.

Who told you that your eyes are not to be trusted? That was what Lev had asked me at the school.

"Thank you," I said to my aunt before heading upstairs. I wiped my tears away. Before I went to Marty's room, my uncle called out to me. He had Marcella with him. He invited me in.

"It's okay," I said. "I'm kinda tired." I rushed away to Marty's room, shutting the door behind me. All I wanted to do was stare at that picture. I was fixated by it, almost afraid to even blink, thinking it might vanish.

I went straight to his bed that sat against the window. Lying down, holding the photo above me, I looked up at it.

"So," I whispered to myself. "What does this mean?" It meant that I didn't hallucinate about the lanterns. What I saw in the picture was what I remembered. I wondered why Rita came all that way to give this to me. I looked on the back of the photo and found a message from her. It read:

Hey, Mae, I finally did what you asked me. I found the picture of the man you said you met in the woods. I was too scared to look because it was easier for me to write you off than to question the world around me. I'm so sorry. I am a horrible friend. I don't think you were imagining being out of Eradeem. I don't understand how it could happen, but everything that happened that night was so strange, and I tried to push it out of my mind, but I know that you are right. I hope this picture will remind you that you aren't crazy.

I wasn't expecting that at all. All of a sudden, she believed me. How was that possible? Even though Rita was the only one who was there and saw the lantern in the sky with me, she never seemed to care much about them.

I picked up the envelope, thinking it was empty, but there was something else inside. Another photo, but of the red cardinal. It was taken right before we saw the lanterns. I looked on the back, and it had another message from Rita:

P.S. This bird won't leave me alone. I've seen it almost every day since the night you disappeared. It feels like it's hunting me until I finally just trust that you are right about everything. I hope you can forgive me.'

Tap tap tap. A sound from the window jerked my thoughts back to the room. I looked over, and there at the windowsill was the cardinal.

"What's happening?" I asked.

Was it possible this was the same bird we saw the first time? The bird that was hanging around campus? The cardinal Rita claimed was hunting her? Was it hunting me, too? It tapped its beak against the window, making me jump from the bed. I backed away, feeling uneasy as it cocked its head to the side, looking at me and continuing to peck against the window. "Can birds do that?" I said out loud.

"Mae," my aunt called as she entered the room. "I just got a call from Ms. Vivly. She said she will be here in a couple of hours. I did mention to her about you staying here with me. But I don't think it's going to happen. I'm sorry."

"Oh," I said. "Well, I'd hoped I had more time to be with you guys before getting sent away again."

"Yeah, me, too. She didn't want me to tell you. But I didn't feel right not letting you know. I thought it would give you a couple hours to get your mind right."

"Right," I said, looking back at the window. "Okay, thanks anyway."

"Is that a bird?" my aunt said, walking over to the window. "Wow, I used to see them when I was a kid. But it's strange to see them now. It's red, too."

"I think he's following me," I said, staying away from the window. "That bird was at my school, too."

"I'm sure it's not the same bird. Your grandpa used to tell me and your mother that red birds were good luck."

"Luck?"

"Yeah, he makes up so much stuff, it's hard to believe him. It's a beautiful bird, though. Well, I'll get going so you can be alone for a bit. Let me know if you need anything."

"Right," I replied, but being alone was the last thing I wanted.

Twenty Eight

Once my aunt left, the bird started tapping on the window again. Maybe it was good luck, I thought as I walked over slowly, climbing back into bed to get to the window.

"You again." I stretched my hand to the window, pressing my palm on the glass, where the bird was. It paused, looking right at me.

I reached for the lock and slid it across, slowly lifting the window. I ducked as the bird flew inside. It went directly over to Marty's desk, landed, and then flew out of the window, dropping something on the bed as it went. I reached down to pick up Marty's work badge. It read, "Border Control Sector 12," and had Marty's picture and name on it. It was in a plastic pocket with a key card on the other side. This was the key Marty used for working at the border. I could use it to leave Eradeem.

"Can you understand me?" I said, looking at the cardinal sitting on a tree by the window. I was feeling a bit insane again.

"Are you trying to tell me something?"

I slowly stretched my hand out the window. The cardinal flew immediately to me, landing on my hand.

"No way!"

It took a few hops on my hand to turn and then flew back out of the window as a gust of wind came in, blowing the picture of Lev to the floor. I went over to it, picking it up from the ground with Marty's badge still in my hand.

"Am I supposed to leave Eradeem?"

I looked back out the window to see if the bird was there, but it was gone. Was this really happening? Had a bird just come into this room, trying to persuade me to run away— or was I going mad? Another breeze came, but softer this time, pulling the curtains through the window. If this wasn't a sign, I didn't know what was.

Ms. Vivly was coming for me, and there was no way she would let me stay here with my family. She would send me to a place for crazy people. What did I have to lose? My mother, father, and grandfather were gone, and soon I would be taken away from my aunt. All my friends were gone, and I had no idea what had happened to them. If it was something really bad, it was because of me. "I have nothing left," I said to myself.

I took an empty book bag and a military jacket from Marty's closet. I put on the jacket and place the picture of Lev and the bird in the pocket. It was big on me, but that was good in case it got cold. Walking over to the door, I peeked out, seeing my aunt in the room with my uncle and Marcella. Their backs were turned away from the hall, so I quickly sneaked past them, down the stairs to the kitchen.

I went through the kitchen pantry, putting some food in my bag. I didn't really think about what I was putting inside, but I made sure to get several bottles of water. There was a flashlight nearby, so I took it. I went out the back door so none of the neighbors would notice me. Before taking off, I mapped out the direction I was going in my head, thinking of the fastest way to the wall where Marty had found me.

I thought about where my house was and headed that way, moving quickly. I was out of the neighborhood before I knew it. There was a forested area nearby that was good for staying out of sight. I looked around, making sure no one was watching me before I disappeared into the trees. Once I was inside, out of nowhere, darting straight through the trees like a red arrow, was the cardinal. I realized what it was doing. I began to follow it.

I jumped over logs, dodged trees, and shoved branches aside. Twigs scraped my bare legs. The pain of my bandaged arm was intense, but I pushed through it. Thinking about what Ms. Vivly had planned for me inspired me to run faster. The bird seemed to be flying at a pace that I could keep up with. I didn't know where it was taking me, but I hoped it was the wall.

Several times, I had to slow down to catch my breath, but I never stopped moving. My eyes stayed high so I would not lose track of the cardinal. I felt an incredible sense of joy as I pushed myself harder to keep up. The journey to escape from Eradeem for fear of my life had reminded me of something I'd felt when I was younger: the joy of running free. I let my mind go, feeling the wind in my hair. If this were my last day, I was happy to be where I was.

Although my aunt didn't live as far from the city as we did, she wasn't too far from the border. Before I knew it, I entered the field surrounded by trees. The same field where Grandpa's base was. I could see Grandpa's tiny home. It felt like it was the only thing left of him. I stopped to rest as I hunched over to breathe. The sweat dripped from my forehead to the ground, but my lungs felt so good. I looked over, and just a few steps away from me was my redheaded doll.

I picked it up, shaking off the dirt. I didn't think I would see it again. Looking over the field reminded me of my good memories there. On my fourth birthday, my family had brought me to the field to celebrate, right before Grandma died. That was when she gave me the doll. She wanted the doll's hair to be red like hers. Maybe she knew she wouldn't be alive much longer. I added the doll to my bag, wishing I could go back to that time, but nothing ever stayed the same. I looked back to see the city on the horizon like I had when I'd first left Eradeem. But this time, I wouldn't be back.

The cardinal was already far ahead, but I knew where to go from there. Cutting through the plain, I entered the woods and made my way up a steep hill like before. Once I started to see the wall through the trees, I slowed my pace. The cardinal was nowhere in sight. There was only one guard on watch and no one on the top of the wall like before. The guard's head was buried in a magazine; he probably wasn't used to people trying to cross the wall. I saw the door to his far right. I could easily run through it without being noticed. I was far enough away that he probably couldn't hear me running; I'd just have to be quick.

I put my hand in my pocket, taking hold of the badge. I closed my eyes and took in a deep, slow breath. I started counting down, and when I got to four, I found myself dashing to the wall straight for the door. I took the badge, and I quickly pressed it on the sensor. I heard a click, and I pushed the door open. I closed it swiftly behind me. I leaned against the door, catching my breath, hoping that no one was inside. It was dark, with very dim lighting coming from the ceiling. I could hear voices, but I didn't see anyone. I looked around to be sure.

Right in front of me was another door. I walked over. I couldn't believe how far I had made it. My heart pounded as my palms became sweaty. I used my badge one last time and pushed the door open.

The brightness of the sun overtook my vision. I shielded my eyes with my hands to block the light. As my eyes adjusted, I saw an endless sea of sand and a blue sky. I blinked and rubbed my sight, but the desert was still there. I wasn't sure what I'd expected.

My head became light as I dropped to my knees and stared into the nothingness. This was the desert that separated us from the outside world. Marty told me that outside of this wall was a chemical wasteland, and that the air caused madness. Was I really going to continue? My mind was scrambled, and my thoughts weren't coming to me clearly. I touched the sand, picking it up and letting it fall through my fingers. It was hot. As I stared down at it, a small shadow passed over me. I looked up to see the cardinal above me, flying down and landing in front of me.

"Are…are you real?" I asked, feeling as though my mind was gone. "Why did you bring me here?" I reached out my hand to it. As soon as I did, it jumped up, flapping its wings, and landed on the back of my hand. It took a couple of gentle pecks at my wrist. I brought it closer to me and gently stroked it with my fingers.

"You're not trying to kill me, are you?" The bird flew up to my shoulder, yanking my hair, and then soared off into the desert.

"What are you doing?" I asked myself, throwing my head down. "Do you want to die?"

"No," I answered myself. I was sure that what I was doing was for the best. I stood up slowly, and I began walking forward.

I looked back at the wall of Eradeem. It was the same color as the sand. The only thing across the wall was the tree line of the forest I had been in. There was no one watching me and no one to stop me. It was the cardinal who had led me here. Maybe it was stupid to follow a bird to a desert, but at least I wasn't alone.

The air was drier and hotter. It was always warm in Eradeem, but the heat out here was almost unbearable. I took my jacket off and tied it around my waist. How long could I last out here before dying? The bird was so high it appeared black against the clouds. It tilted side to side as it glided against the wind like a kite, staying in sight as I followed.

I still couldn't understand what had happened that day I first saw the stars. I'd never passed through a desert or a wall. But I kept walking, crying on and off. I tried to stay focused, but my mind kept wandering. At one point, I just let everything go and screamed at the top of my lungs. I felt like a lost child looking for her mother. I was far enough that I could see the whole city from where Eradeem's clouds ended and the blue sky began. I stopped to take a break and pulled out my water. But as I tried to sit, the cardinal came down, flapping its wings in my face and around me. I tried to wave it away, but until I started to walk again, it wouldn't stop.

"Okay!" I shouted. "I won't take a break." I continued drinking my water as I walked. "Crazy bird," I mumbled, glaring at it. I untied my jacket and put it over my head to block the sun. I took another look back, and I could barely see Eradeem. When I'd started, the sun had seemed to be right above me, but it had moved to my side.

I didn't know why I believed that, somehow, I would run into Lev in the desert. But I seemed to be alone, besides the cardinal. I collapsed to the ground; I pulled off my shoes and poured out the sand from them. This time that bird didn't bother me. I'd eaten most of my food, and I had one bottle of water left. I lay back in the sand, staring up at the sky. The cardinal hovered over me and flew down until it landed on my chest. It hopped into my view. "What do you want from me?" I asked. It only stared at me a bit before it flew off. I didn't even bother to see where it went. I was so exhausted. There was no way I was moving. I thought about the last time I'd seen Lev, right before seeing the bird at school. He'd said a lot to me. I didn't really understand it or remember much. But there was one thing he'd said that came back to me.

The rip in the barrier. An invisible barrier that separated him from Eradeem. If it was true, then maybe that was how I was able to pass through the desert last time. Maybe that was why I saw strange animals around where I lived. Maybe that was where the glowing bugs came from. I'd told everyone back at Lukenic that Lev was the ghost at the school, and the king from the story. Was Lev actually a king? Was he a ghost?

I pulled my jacket over my face to block out the sun. "Maybe Lev sent you to me," I whispered to the cardinal. I went through my thoughts, trying to understand. Then the words from one of the lanterns from Grandpa's base came back to me.

Ghost, bird, man, king
To Eradeem, the light they bring
They alone can bring back peace
Once beast beneath has been unleashed

The cardinal, the ghost from school, and the king from Lev's story. Maybe they were all Lev. "There is no such thing as ghosts," I said, chuckling at the thought. Walking past a desert didn't seem possible, but it had happened. I closed my eyes, trying to imagine Lev's face again. I started to think about him finding me in the woods. The sheep he took care of. The cliff we stood on, looking at Eradeem from afar. The fire that sat between us as he told his story, and the warmth of his hands right before I woke up. It was all so strange, but the peace from the memory overtook me. My sadness faded, and I fell asleep.

When I woke, my jacket was still over my face, and it was much cooler than before. I sat up to complete darkness. There was no moon. But as my eyes adjusted, I noticed the sky was lit up. I rubbed my face and blinked a few times. Was I hallucinating, or was I seeing stars again? They covered the sky from one end to the other. I looked behind me to see them stretching as far as I could see. It was just like I remembered. They were beautiful. I was surprised to see them but bewildered at the same time. I stood, grabbing my bag to pull out the flashlight. My light hit a tree that was just ahead of me. "I don't remember seeing that before."

I made my way to it and saw my bird friend resting on the branches. I smiled at it as I pulled a leaf from a branch to examine it. It wasn't like I'd never seen a tree before, but I was curious how a tree could survive in the desert. I looked past the tree and saw in the distance that the sand had long grass sticking up from it. As I tried to scan the sand in the distance, my eyes caught something else.

"No way," I said out loud. Coming from the dark horizon were lights flowing up to the night sky. They looked so far away, but I could see exactly what they were.

"Am I really seeing this?" I said, rubbing my eyes.

Maybe the chemicals in the desert were making me hallucinate. But I'd come this far, and there was no turning back at this point.

The cardinal chirped and then took off toward the glowing lights. I went back to find my shoes and put them on. As I shined my flashlight, I couldn't see the bird anymore. All in front of me were the lanterns. So, I ran after them, following their trail.

*****

Acknowledgments

With sincere gratitude, I would like to thank my family and friends who have helped bring this book into form.

My best friend, Gabrielle Solange, you are indispensable in this project. You gave the book its name and without you, Where the Stars Hide would never had made it out of my head. Thank you for having suffered through my first drafts, being my number one fan, creating interior art for the book, and calling me a writer to the world when I was afraid to call it out to myself.

My mother, Carla James. You were the first person to see me as a writer in my depressed teenage years. I thank you so much for being so encouraging in my youth, for having big dreams, and setting the foundations for making me want more in life.

My husband, Afzal Gulzar, who took my mother's place in making me dream big. Thank you for making me see possibilities in places I would never have believed in without your companionship. You've changed how I see the world, and you hold me accountable for what I set out to do. Without you, I would remain complacent.

To my friends, Qwentin Hill, Samuel Hougland, and Kelsea Gifford. Thank you for your critique of Where the Stars Hide. You've helped me improve the story. I appreciate you all for putting in the time to read my book to help me bring it to where it is now. It means everything to me.

Last but not least, I thank God for giving me Where the Stars Hide. You are my true inspiration. Everything I've ever done that's worthy of greatness can only be credited to when I accepted you in my life. I am so grateful for you, and I have no regrets.

ABOUT THE AUTHOR

Patricia Gulzar is a born storyteller who uses her imagination as a tool to escape depression, create new worlds, and explain complex ideas. She is an analytical, dyslexic, no-nonsense dreamer who surrounds herself with amazing friends and family, whom she loves to add to her stories.

When she isn't creating new worlds, she is hosting her YouTube channel, cooking for her Pakistani husband, and seeking the next anime romance to binge.

Patricia Gulzar lives in Columbus, Ohio, where she runs Write the Truth Productions, LLC, and is the CEO of Gulzar Properties, LLC, a nonprofit real estate organization that provides affordable housing for all demographics stuck in the wealth gap. For more information on Patricia, you can visit Patriciagulzar.com.